THE ADVENTURES OF
GRAVEDIGGER
VOLUME ONE

by BARRY REESE

THE ADVENTURES OF GRAVEDIGGER
A Reese Unlimited Book
Published by Pro Se Press

"Gravedigger" & "Grave Matters Or... How I Came To Write This Book", and "Timeline" Copyright © 2013, Barry Reese

Cover Art and "Gravedigger" Logo by George Sellas, Interior Illustrations by Will Meugniot.

Print Production and Book Design by Sean E. Ali
E-Book Design by Russ Anderson

Edited by David White

Pro Se Productions, LLC
133 1/2 Broad Street
Batesville, AR, 72501
870-834-4022

proseproductions@earthlink.net
www.prosepulp.com

THE ADVENTURES OF
GRAVEDIGGER
VOLUME ONE

THE ADVENTURES OF GRAVEDIGGER VOLUME ONE

TABLE of CONTENTS

THE SOVEREIGN
CITY PROJECT ™

PROLOGUE

The Hessian spat out the blood that filled his mouth, hefting his saber for another attack. He was standing in ankle-deep mud, his uniform stained with grime and gore, and the men he faced were poorly trained Revolutionaries. Their main advantage was the fact that they knew the territory well but the Hessian also knew that a man fighting for his home and family was given extra strength and ferocity.

The Hessian roared, stepping over the severed limb of one of his compatriots. He approached an opponent from behind, reaching around with his blade to slit the man's throat so deeply that the head was only attached to the body by a thin strip of gristle.

The rain had begun again and the roar of thunder, coupled with the sounds of battle all around, made it hard for the Hessian to focus. He dodged the thrust of a young man's bayonet before finishing the youth with the point of his sword.

It was moments like these that filled the Hessian with joy. Unlike many of his fellows, he had volunteered for service, rather than being conscripted by Landgrave Frederick II. He was a soldier in wartime and a killer in peacetime. The names mattered little to him. He had grown up the youngest of six bloodthirsty brothers, trained to be rabid murderers by their drunk of a father. The only thing that the Hessian enjoyed as much as battle was sex, and both were done with equal amounts of violence and glee.

He whirled about, eager to kill again. He was not a handsome man and he currently looked even more nightmarish than usual. His longish hair was caked with blood and his right eye, marred by a small scar that ran underneath the bottom lid, was bloodshot and slightly bulging. Earlier in the battle, he had come into close quarters with an enemy, biting off the man's earlobe. Now blood stained his teeth and dripped from the corners of his mouth.

He saw the enemy on the hill, packing one of their cannons for another shot. They were a motley group and their weapons misfired as often as they worked. But the Hessian knew that his own regiment was not faring well. Of the 80 men they had begun this battle with, less than a fourth were still standing.

Charging towards the hill, the Hessian hacked his way through those in his path, friend and foe alike. A well placed shot from that cannon could end the battle and he could not allow that. He screamed a German battle cry and then stopped in his tracks, eyes wide. It was too late, the cannon's fuse had run out.

An explosion of fire and smoke accompanied the launching of the cannonball. It soared straight towards the Hessian, who was suddenly frozen with the realization that his life of brutality was about to end. The cannon smashed right through his skull, leaving his body standing in place. It twitched and danced for a long moment, as if it hadn't quite realized yet that its head was gone. The torso twisted and the hands reached out, as if in hopes that it could find its missing top.

The Hessian's body spun about and crashed to the mud, coming to rest no more than four feet from the remains of his head, which smoldered in the rain.

PART ONE
THE RISING DARK

Chapter I
Little Dead Girl

October 31, 1936

*T*his is not a decision entered into lightly. It is a tremendous gesture of faith that you are about to receive.

There was a pause before The Voice continued. Charity stirred within the casket, fear beginning to mount within her. How long had she been buried beneath the earth? How much air was left to her?

You will have three years in which to redeem your soul. Find those who are unfit for the world of mortals and destroy them: man or demon, the enemy of the innocent is now your enemy. You will put them into their graves and shovel upon them the dirt that symbolizes their eviction from this plane of existence.

On Halloween Night, 1939, you will be called back to this place and you will be judged for a final time. If your soul has been made pure, you will find your reward. If your soul is still tainted black... Your suffering will never know an end.

Do you accept these terms? Do you want to live?

Charity had forced the words out, ignoring the pain it caused her. Her throat was dry and raw. "Yes. Yes! I want to live."

So be it.

January 1937

*H*ector Martinez was nervous. He was smoking his fifth cigarette in the last hour and his hands were shaking. He paced back and forth outside his ramshackle home, located deep in a crime-ridden area of Sovereign City.

The nighttime sky was cloudy and the smell of fresh rain lingered in his nostrils, mixing with other, more unpleasant odors. Locals joked that a day without rain in Sovereign was like a cat without a tail – you saw one on occasion but it was a rare thing, indeed.

The door behind him opened and closed. Julio, three years Hector's senior and the oldest of all the family's sons, bore a large grin beneath his handlebar moustache. He laughed when he saw Hector's anxiety, writ large on his little brother's face. "It's done little brother. No more worry, si?"

"We shouldn't have done this," Hector replied. He threw down his cigarette and ground it out beneath his shoe. "We get caught and we're going to fry in the state pen."

"Nobody saw us take her," Julio said, taking on a more serious expression. He put his hands on his brother's shoulders and pulled him close, staring into his eyes. "If you keep your mouth shut, we'll never get caught."

"Her body…?"

"Burned. Along with all her clothes. It's like she was never here."

Hector exhaled, breaking away from his brother's gaze. "God will never forgive me for this."

"You are a man, mi hermano. We see what we want and we take it."

"But she was just a child," Hector said, feeling ashamed as hot tears began to burn to his eyes. He could see Rosalita at play, skipping rope in her Sunday dress. She was only six years old but he'd coveted her smooth skin and dark eyes. He'd never acted on his desires for children before, but on this day, he'd succumbed to his dark lust. He'd grabbed her and dragged her away, tying her up in his home. The rape had gone quickly but in the aftermath he'd been so scared and ashamed that he hadn't been sure what to do. He'd called his brother because Julio always took care of him.

To his surprise, Julio hadn't been shocked in the least by what he found at his brother's house. He'd told Hector go outside and leave him alone with the girl, who was still alive but very quiet.

Hector had ignored everything from that point forward: the sounds of struggle, the brief cry that was quickly snuffed out, even the horrible smells that drifted from the large oven in his home. Julio had handled it all, every disgusting detail, and Hector loved him for it.

Julio reached out and touched his brother's chin, tilting his head back up. "No more talking about it, si? It's over. If anyone comes by asking about anything, you tell them to talk to me."

"You are too good to me," Hector said.

"We are family."

Something moved in the shadows and Hector jumped.

"What is it?" Julio asked, looking about.

"I thought I saw someone."

Julio stared into the gloom but he could see nothing. There were few streetlamps in this area of the city and the darkness was almost like a living thing, growing in size as the midnight hour drew near. "It's just your nerves."

Hector started to reply but his words twisted into a squawk of terror as a figure leaped from the night, landing beside Julio. It was a woman, dressed in a form-fitting red and black bodysuit. Weapons of all type were fastened about her body and she held a curved Arabian-style sword in her right hand. Her face was hidden beneath a black facemask and hood, adding to her mystery.

Julio never knew what hit him. He had scarcely realized the reason for his brother's terror when the woman had begun to swing her sword in a deadly arc. It cut through Julio's neck, decapitating him in one fell swoop.

Hector emitted a high-pitched scream and took off running, the sight of his brother's head flying through the air etched into his mind's eye. He sprinted into the darkness, not knowing or caring where he was going. This was God's Vengeance, manifested in human form. Or was it Rosalita's spirit, come to claim her revenge?

The wraith-like woman was suddenly in front of him. Hector tried to stop but he lost his balance and tumbled to the ground, rolling until he was almost at her feet.

The woman knelt in a smooth motion, catching Hector's throat between two blades – the curved sword with which she'd killed his brother and a smaller knife that gleamed in the moonlight.

"Please!" he begged, feeling the cold touch of the weapons. One of them pricked just deep enough to draw blood.

"Did you listen when Rosalita begged?" the woman said. Her voice was as cold as the steel she wielded.

Hector closed his eyes. "Madre de dios, please forgive me."

"There is no forgiveness for you."

Hector looked into the woman's mask, as dark as the night that

surrounded them both.

"You dug your own grave, Hector. All I'm doing is shoveling the dirt on top."

Hector's life ended quickly, as the twin blades snipped together, tearing through everything in between.

———∽∞∞∽———

Gravedigger stood up, pulling a dark cloth from one of the pouches on her waist. She cleaned her weapons and sheathed them. There was no joy in her heart over this victory. She had arrived too late to save the girl, despite her best efforts to trace her kidnapper. But she'd heard enough of the brothers' discussion to know what had to be done.

She left the corpses where they lay, entering the house and examining the oven's contents. Julio hadn't been quite as good as his word – there were plenty of bones that were identifiably human, as well as scraps of cloth that came from the girl's dress and underwear.

Again her hands darted down into the pouches at her belt. She retrieved a miniaturized walkie-talkie and turned it on. Static filled the room but she depressed the talk button and said, "You can contact the police. Send them to 142 Bloch Avenue."

"Any survivors?" a man asked in reply. His words were spoken with a clipped British accent, which always surprised people in Sovereign when they saw him. Mitchell was a massive black man with a shaved head and a menacing face. But he had been born in London and had a heart of gold.

"No."

Mitchell heard the sound of disappointment in Gravedigger's voice. "You can't blame yourself for this, luv. Nothing can undo that little girl's death but at least you made her killers pay."

"I'm sure that will help her parents sleep at night."

"It just might."

Gravedigger ceased communications and put the walkie-talkie away. She knew that Mitchell would be along soon, driving his plain, unmarked sedan. She didn't feel like talking any more about this but she had a feeling he wasn't going to let the matter drop.

A calendar on the wall caught her attention. Someone had drawn red x's through all the days of the month, all the way to today. A chill ran down her spine before she whirled about and left the house. Time was like an unstoppable juggernaut. Every second grew into minutes, then hours, then days.

Three years was not so much.

Chapter II
Everyone Has Secrets

Josef Goldstein wore a dark suit and an open-necked white shirt. He was a thin old man with round glasses, thinning hair and a trim white beard that framed a wide mouth. He leaned heavily on a walking stick as he moved through his house, a large red ruby shining on his ring finger. "Charity?" he called. "Are you up?"

"I'm in here," she answered.

Goldstein ambled into the room that had become Charity's personal gymnasium. She was doing chin-ups with a bar attached to one of the walls, her athletic form glistening with sweat. She wore loose-fitting pants and an undershirt. Her shoulder-length brown hair was tied back into a ponytail and her eyes, chocolate brown, regarded Goldstein coolly

"Mitchell says that you were upset about the mission last night."

"Mitchell has a big mouth."

Goldstein found a chair and sat down heavily. Charity continued her exercise routine. "You're doing quite well, you know."

"Why? Because I've killed ten people in the past three months?"

"Twelve, actually. You always forget Big Eddy and his friend."

Charity dropped to the floor and put her hands on her hips. "What do you want?" she asked testily.

Goldstein smiled softly, revealing a set of teeth that were a little too perfect. They were fake and, to Charity's eyes, were indicative of his entire persona. "If you ever want to talk about things, I'm here for you. Like I told you on the night we met, I was once a Gravedigger myself. I know the stresses that you're under."

Charity nodded, as if remembering something. "Oh, yes, the night we met. I think that was when you shot me and buried me alive, wasn't it?"

Goldstein's smile widened. "I killed you, Charity. You know that."

"I don't know what happened," Charity responded, turning away from him. She picked up a couple of weights and began doing a set of repetitions with them.

"You accepted The Voice's offer. Just like I did. Just like all the Gravediggers have done, one after another. But you're the first woman to ever receive the honor."

Charity paused in her actions. "The honor?" she repeated, quietly. "How many Gravediggers passed the test, Goldstein? How many were pure after three years of murder and mayhem?"

"I was judged worthy."

"And how many others?"

"I can't say."

"Can't or won't?" Charity sighed. "It doesn't matter. It is what is." Resuming her workout, she asked, "Are you just here to counsel me or do you have something else to talk about?"

"There's someone else in Sovereign who needs your attention."

Charity set the weights down on the ground and wandered over to where Goldstein was sitting. She preferred it when they talked business. It was the same with Mitchell, though she knew he was a nice guy. Goldstein, though, she wasn't sure about.

She was discovering that she had a tendency to hold grudges against men who tried to kill her.

Goldstein reached into his jacket and pulled out a newspaper clipping. He unfolded it and handed it to Charity. It was from the society section and showed a rather smug looking man shaking hands with the mayor. "That," Goldstein said, "is Arthur Meeks."

"I've heard of him," she answered. "He runs a dairy plant, right?"

"That's where his fortune comes from, yes. He's the chief supplier of milk not just for Sovereign but also for most of the surrounding tri-state area. That's not what concerns us, however. Our focus should be on his unusual interest in rare books. He has spent a considerable amount of money acquiring a series of grimoires that would be the envy of anyone outside of The Illuminati."

Charity sat on the floor, looking up at Goldstein. "I'm still hearing the 'evil' part of things."

"Are you familiar with The Necronomicon?"

Charity looked at him in annoyance. "I'm 23 years old. I was a bright but not particularly great student in school. Do you really think I've heard of something called The Necronomicon?"

"Fair enough," he conceded. "According to the most trustworthy sources, it was originally called *Al Azif*, which translates as 'the howling of demons.' A mad Arab named Alhazred, who worshipped several dark gods, wrote the book after travelling far and wide to learn foul secrets. It was translated into Greek and then Latin, spreading like wildfire through the occult community. In the year 1050, an attempt was made by the Catholic Church to put the work to rest. Copies were rounded up and burned, however several slipped through and were placed into hiding and survived. For many years, it was believed that no copies of the original Arabic version remained... but now Meeks has come into possession of one. This book is indescribably dangerous! The mere study of it is bad enough but any attempt to master its secrets could prove catastrophic, not just for the student... but for the entire world."

"So you want me to kill him... over a book?"

Goldstein narrowed his eyes. "It is not just any book. Did you not listen to me?"

"Has he done anything with it? Has he performed human sacrifices? Is he planning to blow up a church?" Charity stood up and dropped the newspaper clipping into Goldstein's lap. "I'm not going to kill him based on some rumor you've heard about him owning a forbidden book."

"It is not a rumor! I have sources that have—"

"Sources that you never seem to share with me."

"I have told you... Since my time as Gravedigger, I have cultivated connections with many people, in my walks of life. Because when my time of penance was done, I still wanted to help! I still wanted to serve! And that is why I am with you, now. So that I can offer you assistance! I don't want you wasting as much time as I did, trying to find leads. I can bring them to you!"

Charity took a deep breath. "I'm sorry, Josef. I just get so... frustrated."

Goldstein softened his expression. "I understand. Like you, I had lived a lifetime of sin. Neither of us were murderers or beyond redemption... but we had broken many laws, both moral and legal. To have a mirror placed before your very soul, to see how far down you had fallen... and then be told that you have a finite amount of time to correct it all...."

A smile touched Charity's lips. It was so sweet that Goldstein lost his train of thought. This young beauty had not had an easy life and it had hardened her beyond her years. To look at her now, though, was to get a glimpse into the kind of person she could have been, had things done along a different path.

As quickly as that grin had appeared, it had vanished. When Charity looked at him, her expression was cynical and hard, as it usually was. "He's keeping this book in his house, right?"

"Yes."

"Then that's where I'll be going tonight."

"Don't play with him. Just strike quickly and get away. That's what you should have done with those men last night. Instead, you skulked about in the shadows until you heard their confession."

"You have your sources, Josef, but I'm not ready to trust them – or you – 100%. I do this my way." Charity stood up. "I'm going to break into his house and have a look around. Besides, if he's as dirty as you make him sound, I bet this isn't the only pot he's stuck his fingers into. We might need more information if we want to shut down his entire operation."

Goldstein merely nodded as she exited the room. Taking a deep breath, he hoped that she could find a way to silence the anger raging within her.

If not, the next three years would be for naught.

Chapter III
Charity's Life... And Death

Charity Grace had grown up in one of the most squalid sections of Sovereign City, an area known as Ferguson Point. Though her mother had sought to shield her from the truth, she'd eventually learned the facts about her birth. Her mother had been a woman of the night, a peddler of her own flesh. Catching the eye of a wealthy philanthropist, she'd become his mistress and eventually gave birth to a daughter. Fearing the effect this could have on his marriage and family, Charity's father had abandoned the relationship.

The only proof of her heritage lay in the name given to her on her birth certificate: Grace.

Once she'd learned the truth, Charity had become obsessed with her half-sister, a girl named Samantha. She'd seen the girl in the Society pages from time to time, winning a tennis tournament or placing high in some academic bowl.

All of that, Charity realized, could have been – should have been – hers.

Eventually, she'd fallen in with a rough crowd, losing her heart to a roughneck by the name Mack Winslow. When she'd spilled the beans about her father, he'd taken it upon himself to launch a blackmail scheme. In the end, a man named Lazarus Gray had intervened, saving the Grace family from scandal.

Charity had been furious at the turn of events. Not only had her secret been used to harm others but also, Samantha had ended up as a member of Gray's Assistance Unlimited.

After the death of her mother, Charity had been forced to make a difficult decision: Should she confront her father and beg for his assistance? Or should she find some way, any way, of fending for herself.

Given the fact that her father still hadn't come looking for her in the wake of the blackmail scheme, she chose the latter.

Refusing to become a prostitute, she instead became a petty thief. She'd done well enough to find an apartment of her own but beyond that, life was a meager existence.

All of that had changed the night she'd broken into the home of Josef Goldstein. He had just moved into the Gibson Avenue area and, according to the moving men that she'd befriended, wouldn't be actually occupying the place for several days yet.

If all had gone according to her plan, she would have had plenty of time to ransack the many boxes she'd seen carried into the home.

But life was never simple for Charity.

———— ❧ ————

It had taken less than five minutes for her to get inside his house. Armed with only a small flashlight, she had moved through the darkened rooms. Now and then, she had stopped and opened a box, using a small knife on her person. The contents of the packages were enough to set her heart fluttering: expensive jewelry, lovely vases and silk sheets.

A sudden thought had occurred to her: why was Goldstein moving into this neighborhood? With this kind of money, he could have moved into one of the more upscale areas with ease. Maybe, she mused, the stories she'd heard about Jewish people were true: that they were skinflints.

In general, she didn't buy into racial stereotypes. There were several blacks that lived in the apartments around hers and they were nothing like the minstrels that they were portrayed as in newspaper cartoons. On the other hand, the only Jewish person she knew was Mr. Stiller, who owned the local grocery, and he certainly embodied all the negatives she'd heard about his race.

Charity had stepped into the living room and stopped, letting her light travel up the fireplace and over the painting that hung above. It was a marvelous piece of work, though its subject matter sent a chill down her spine: a cloaked figure on horseback, a scythe held in one hand. It was Death, riding his black steed, with the souls of the damned writhing in torment along the sides of the road.

"A moving image, is it not?"

Charity had jumped, spinning about so quickly that she nearly dropped her flashlight. Her free hand had stealthily retrieved her knife from its place on her hip and she brandished it with obvious experience.

Illuminated by her light was an old man, sitting in a plush-backed chair. He wore a dark suit and a white shirt that was open at the collar. His glasses had reflected the light back at her. He had thinning hair and a white beard that framed a wide mouth. His right hand was balanced on a walking stick and a large red ruby adorned his ring finger. "My name is Josef Goldstein. But I think you might know that all ready, yes?"

Charity had sighed, lowering her weapon. She wasn't averse to violence when it was necessary but she wasn't prepared to come to blows with an old man. If it meant another stint in the lockup, she would take her medicine. She had been in and out of the prison system over the last couple of years and it didn't scare her any longer.

"Cat got your tongue?" Goldstein prodded.

"What can I say?" Charity had answered. "You caught me."

"And that's all you have to offer? No explanations? No pleas for leniency?" Goldstein stood up, his bones creaking. "You look like a child."

"I'm older than I look." Charity had moved the light away from his face, letting it fall against his chest. "Why are you here in the dark?"

"I like the dark. A man can sometimes see more in the dark than he can in the light."

Charity had put away her knife, her shoulders sagging. "Should I wait here while you flag down a police car? They usually patrol this street every twenty minutes or so."

"No. I don't think we'll need to involve the authorities." Goldstein stepped past her, moving slowly towards one of the boxes she had opened. It contained a number of old books but nothing that had caught her eye as particularly valuable. "Do you believe in the afterlife, Charity?"

"I used to read the bible but I don't... Wait. How did you know my name?"

Goldstein bent over and rifled through the box, pushing aside the books. "Once I was like you," he continued, ignoring her question. "I lived my life, obsessed with things of the physical world. I broke the law repeatedly, under the misguided belief that I was simply doing what I had to do to survive. And then one day I met an old woman, who showed me the secret path."

Charity glanced back towards the window. If she fled now, she might be able to get away with this. No cops, no prison... Of course, he did seem to know her name.

"My dear?"

Charity shone the light upon Mr. Goldstein. He held a gun in his free hand. "Mr. Goldstein," she began, suddenly realizing that this old man was more dangerous than she'd first thought. "I'm sorry... I just thought I could make a little bit of money off some of your things! I wasn't going to take much!"

Goldstein smiled toothily. "Well, now, that sounds more like what I was expecting." He tilted his head to the side. "I apologize for this. It will seem very cruel but when next we meet, you'll understand what a great gift I've given you. It's why I came here, out of all the places in America. I came here because of *you*."

Charity had screamed as Goldstein pulled the trigger. His weapon spat out death and it struck home in her chest, knocking her back.

She was dead before her body hit the floor.

———⟡———

The Voice awakened her. Lying scared in a pine box, she had listened to its strange offer... and she had eagerly accepted it, preferring any kind of life to a certain death.

She had fought her way free, calling upon strength that she never knew she possessed. Up, through, the earth, fingers bleeding, she had pushed onward, until finally her hand had broken through to the surface. With a long, low grunt, she had pulled herself up and out, sprawling onto her back, taking massive breaths of air.

How long she lay there under the stars, she didn't know. Eventually, she became aware that someone was with her and she pulled herself up to a kneeling position. She wasn't surprised that it was Goldstein, leaning heavily on his cane. He was smiling, showing his mouthful of perfect teeth.

"I knew you would accept the offer," he said. "You're a fighter."

"Water," she gasped, rising unsteadily.

Goldstein reached into his expensive jacket and pulled forth a silver flask, of the kind that men might carry liquor in. He passed it to her and nodded as she unscrewed the cap and downed the water in three massive gulps. "We should go back to my home. You're welcome to live there with me but if you prefer, it can be a temporary thing."

Charity looked around at the rows of grave markers. This was

Sovereign City's largest cemetery and it was rumored that the pink-tinged mist that clung to visitors'' ankles was actually caused by all the evil of those buried here, seeping up through the ground. Charity had always thought that was nonsense but now she wasn't so sure. She did know that Doc Daye buried the corpses of his worst enemies in this cemetery, which tended to lend credence to the old wives' tale.

"You said you came to Sovereign because of me," Charity said at last. "What does that mean?"

"Exactly what it sounds like, my dear. Remember when I told that you I'd been in your situation once? I, too, was a Gravedigger. And now it is my responsibility to find others who could benefit in the same way that I did."

"Gravedigger?" Charity remembered what The Voice had said: *You will put them into their graves and shovel upon them the dirt that symbolizes their eviction from the mortal world.* "Is that what I am now? A Gravedigger?"

"Yes. The first woman ever to hold such an honor."

"I've been in fights before... but I'm not Lazarus Gray or somebody like that. I can't do those things."

"Yes, you can. You fought your way out of the ground, didn't you? You're stronger, faster and tougher than you were before. And you should be fearless. You know that you're not going to die, not for at least another three years."

Charity looked down at her ruined clothing. "I can't go through town like this."

"You won't have to. I have a car parked just outside and there is a change of clothes for you inside. You don't have to worry about whether or not they'll fit. They're yours."

"You went into my apartment?"

"My associate, Mitchell, did. That's him over there."

Charity squinted through the gloom, where she saw a broad shouldered black man standing in front of a large oak tree. He wore a dark suit and his head was shaved bald but his expression was one of openness. She turned back to Goldstein, studying him closely.

"Is something wrong?" he asked.

"You killed me. I'm just wondering why I'm not angrier about that."

"You've been through a lot. And there's more to come, I'm afraid. Mitchell and I will be in charge of training you. We have so much to do... and only three short years to do it in."

"Gravedigger," Charity said, letting the word roll around in her head.

Goldstein looked sad for a moment, as if the word evoked memories that were painful to him. "Yes."

"I'm going to kill a lot of people, aren't I?"

The old man's expression changed, becoming one full of dark humor. "Oh, yes," he chuckled. "But they'll deserve it, each and every one."

"I just don't know if I can do that. I'm not a murderer."

Goldstein shook his head. "My dear girl, you would be shocked at the things a person can learn to do." Changing the subject, the old man said, "I know about your father. I know about your dreams. So much that belongs to Samantha Grace could have been yours. And now you've been given a chance to seize the brass ring! To change your entire world!"

"And I'll do this by killing people?" Charity asked, her heart hammering in her chest.

"It's a start."

"These will be your weapons. Each belonged to a Gravedigger before you. You will add to the arsenal over time, as well, and then those weapons will be passed down to those who follow you." Goldstein was leaning on his cane, standing behind a table whose surface was hidden beneath a mound of blades. "Choose whatever calls to you."

Dressed in a white turtleneck and dark green slacks, Charity didn't look like an angel of retribution this morning. She had slept hard and then wolfed down a delicious breakfast that Mitchell had prepared. Goldstein had watched her eat in silence but as soon as the last morsel of food had passed her lips, he had sprung into action, asking her to follow him into one of the many rooms of his home.

Charity reached out and lifted up a curved blade. Its highly polished surface gleamed in the sunlight that drifted in through the windows. She stepped back and spun it through the air with ease, the weapon whistling. She paused, eyes wide. "I feel like I've used this before."

"Trace memories," Goldstein replied. "You received them when you accepted The Voice's offer. You'll find that you can accomplish many things just by trying them."

Charity plucked up a small crossbow and studied it. It was fitted with a band so that it could be tied about her wrist. She affixed it and whirled, operating the firing mechanism by a delicate movement of her arm. The bolt shot forth and buried itself in the exact spot where she'd intended it to go.

"Don't get cocky," Goldstein warned. "A lot of what you're doing at the moment is based upon instinct. But when you have a bullet whizzing past your head, you might find yourself freezing up. You have to learn to be the same in battle that you are in practice."

Charity removed the mini crossbow from her wrist and set it back on the table. Lowering her voice, she said, "You called it The Voice. That's what I think of it as, too. Who is it? God?"

"Perhaps it is Adonai – that is what we Jews call the Lord in our prayers – but I personally think that it is not the God of the holy book. What relationship The Voice has with the most holy, I cannot fathom. It is what it is."

"But you're still religious? You still pray to… Adonai?"

"Of course. The Voice has never complained so why shouldn't I keep all sides happy?" Goldstein laughed at his own joke. "Tell me, Charity, are you a religious person? Is that why you're asking these questions?"

"My mother used to read to me out of the bible but that's the extent of it. I never believed in God. After The Voice, though, maybe I should."

Goldstein took a deep breath. "We should begin. You have a finite amount of time, after all."

Charity opened her mouth to say something when a powerful set of arms locked around her throat, nearly crushing her windpipe. Stars formed quickly in front of her eyes and Goldstein stood by, doing nothing.

Mitchell's voice, doom and firm, echoed in her ear. "I don't want to do it but I'll kill you if you don't fight back."

The pounding in her head was almost overwhelming now but Charity felt no fear. There was a mountain of resolve within her that she was just beginning to recognize. She had died once – and, according to The Voice, she would not die again… at least not for another three years. Somehow, someway, she would find a way out of this.

With confidence blooming, Charity threw her body back, raising both feet off the ground. She set them against the edge of the table and then shoved with all her might, sending bladed weapons skittering across the floor and driving Mitchell off-balance. He held on tight but the two of them ended up against the wall.

Charity reached behind her with her right hand, grabbing hold of Mitchell's crotch. She squeezed hard enough to elicit a scream of pain and a loosening of the man's grip. Then she was free of him, dropping into a crouch. A sword was beside her hand and she snatched it up, brandishing it with relish. She rushed Mitchell, who dodged her first swipe and caught her in the back with a hard punch. Her kidneys ached and she felt a scream die in her throat.

Mitchell grabbed her by her hair and yanked her head back. She saw him poised to deliver a punch directly to her face but she struck first, grabbing hold of her sword's hilt with both hands and jamming it back. It slid between two of his ribs and she yanked it free, intending to strike again if need be.

"Enough!" Goldstein shouted and Mitchell released his hold on Charity. He was bent over, one hand pressed tightly against his side. Blood was oozing from between his fingers, dripping onto the floor.

Charity relaxed. She felt no guilt over the man's injury – he had attacked her and deserved no less. She felt a strange sense of calm throughout her being, as if being in combat were her natural state.

Mitchell regarded her with no malice. He grinned, displaying a gold tooth in the upper front. "You move like quicksilver," he said. To Charity's surprise, he had a British accent.

Seeing her expression, Mitchell laughed, wincing as he did so. "Born and raised in Leeds," he explained. "Goldstein, old chap, a little assistance, if you would?"

Goldstein helped Mitchell find a seat and he then directed Charity to fetch his black bag from the other room. After she returned, Goldstein helped open Mitchell's shirt and began to examine the wound.

"Does he need a doctor?" Charity asked.

"I've suffered worse paper cuts than this," Mitchell teased. "Don't beat yourself up over this, luv. It's just training."

"I wasn't," Charity responded. She and Mitchell stared at each other for a moment and then both grinned. "So," she said to Goldstein as he reached for a needle and thread. "Since I broke this one, who's going to be my new sparring partner?"

Mitchell spoke up. "Girl, I'm nowhere near broken."

Charity's smile widened. "Yet."

Goldstein shook his head. "What have I done by bringing the two of you together?"

"When I'm stitched up," Mitchell said, "We'll go again, luv."

"Are you going to be brave enough to face me head on, this time?" Charity strode over to the table and set it back upright. She then picked through the weapons, choosing ones that suited her.

She was just about finished when she caught sight of a box lying open on the floor. It had been hidden from sight behind the table before she'd cause such a mess.

Without asking Goldstein about it, she hurriedly moved over and reached inside. A black and red bodysuit, slightly military in appearance lay within. Underneath were a full-face mask, boots, a shawl and a small clasp that featured the image of a scythe.

"This is mine, isn't it?" she asked, turning her head to look at Goldstein. The old man nodded and she lifted the uniform out of the box. "It's... lovely."

"When I wore it," Goldstein said, "It looked a bit different. They always do, based on what sort of Gravedigger you are."

"You make it sound like you didn't have it made for me," she murmured.

"I didn't. It arrived on my doorstep at dawn this morning. When I became Gravedigger, I found my suit hanging in my closet when I went back home."

Charity eyed the fabric with something akin to hunger. "I have to try it on." She stuffed the uniform back into the box and marched out of the room with it.

After she was gone, Mitchell asked, "You think she's suited for this? I mean, a girl—"

"That girl is going to be incredibly dangerous," Goldstein countered. "The female of the species is always more deadly than the male."

Chapter IV
The Man With the Book

Arthur Meeks sat back, like a king on his throne. He wore only an elaborate Oriental robe that was open in the front, his well-toned body glistening with sweat. He held a glass of vodka in one hand and an opium pipe in the other. The thick smoke that filled the room seemed to shift and move of its own accord, as if it were a living creature.

The room in which Meeks sat was shrouded in darkness, illuminated only by several thick candles that were positioned in each corner. Drapes over the windows kept out all exterior light and emphasized the shadowy surroundings that Meeks preferred.

"Nice place."

Meeks smiled, lifting the pipe to his mouth. He inhaled deeply and held the smoke in his lungs before releasing it.

With heavy-lidded eyes, he glanced towards a spot near the door. The darkness seemed particularly thick there and as he watched, it coalesced into the form of a swarthy man, dressed all in black. The man looked to be of Middle Eastern descent, with a neatly trimmed beard and dark eyes. As he approached, Arthur couldn't help but think that the man looked like an ancient Egyptian Pharaoh, so regal was his bearing.

"I'm so glad to see you," Meeks said with sincerity.

"I appreciate your kindness, Mr. Meeks."

"Call me Arthur," he insisted.

"Very well… Arthur."

Meeks drained the last of his alcohol and tossed the glass to the floor, giggling as it shattered. He looked up at his guest, spittle flying from his lips. "I'm going to treat the world just like that! Boom!"

The dark man lowered his chin, studying Meeks with a malevolent glare. "You would, wouldn't you? You'd sell out your entire race to my masters."

"Gladly," Meeks answered with more than a trace of bitterness. "What has the world ever done for me? Nothing!"

"We need to gather a few more objects of power and then all will be in readiness," the stranger stated. "I am bound in this matter. I cannot touch them. Only the hands of man can gather them."

"I'm working on getting them," Meeks answered. "I found the book, didn't I?"

"Yes, you did. But the next two items won't be as easy. You bought the book but these things aren't for sale."

Meeks puffed away again on the pipe. "Do you have a name?" he asked. "I need something to call you."

"I've gone by many names. I think Mr. Black will do for now."

"Mr. Black," Meeks savored the name. "Will the Old Ones reward me for my service?"

"You will get what has been promised to you: power, wealth and all the slaves you could want."

Meeks stood up, setting his pipe down. He closed his robe and exhaled, a placid smile on his face. "What are these objects that I need to retrieve?"

"One of them is in the Sovereign Museum of Natural History. It's an urn that dates back to Roman times."

"Why would we need an urn?"

"It was used in various dark rituals and retains a substantial amount of power." Mr. Black continued, the expression on his face warning Meeks not to interrupt again. "The other object belongs to a man named Josef Goldstein. He, too, is here in this city. It's a stone, set in a ring." Black's smile returned. "Strange how things come together, isn't it?"

Meeks strode towards the door. "Does it matter which one I go after first?"

A strange look passed over Mr. Black's face but Meeks didn't see it. "I'd start with Goldstein. I have a feeling the old man might be alone this evening."

When night fell upon Sovereign City, a harsh rain that battered against the windows of Goldstein's home accompanied it. He stood in his den, staring out at the street. His face bore a pensive expression and he clutched the head of his cane with ferocious strength.

Mitchell and Charity were gone, leaving him alone in the house. A part of him missed the thrill of the chase, the bloodcurdling thrill of battle... but this was not his time. A new Gravedigger had been named and all he could do was help prepare her for what was to come.

A strange sound reached his ears, making him tense. It was the familiar noise of water dripping onto the floor. Immediately, he knew that he was not alone anymore. There was someone in this room with him and they were watching him, waiting for him to notice their presence.

"I didn't hear you knock," he said.

"That's because I didn't bother."

Goldstein turned slowly, coming face to face with Alan Meeks. The unwelcome visitor wore a long trench coat that was soaked, making it a perfect match for the mop of hair on top of his head. Meeks held a knife in his right hand and his left was glowing slightly, a sign that Goldstein recognized: he had charged his fist with some sort of demonic power.

"What do you want, Mr. Meeks?"

Shock registered briefly on Alan's face. "How do you know my name?"

"I know a lot about you, including the fact that you own the Necronomicon. And from the looks of you, you've already used it to summon at least one of the creatures associated with it." Goldstein took one step forward but stopped when Meeks raised his weapon. "It's not too late to turn back. Put down your knife and I'll do all that I can to help you. I give you my word, Mr. Meeks."

"Don't call me that."

"What would you prefer?"

Meeks grinned madly. "Call me Thanatos."

"The Greek personification of death," Goldstein said. "Very dramatic."

Thanatos laughed hoarsely. "Time to die, old man." He lunged forward, his knife swiping through the air.

Goldstein raised his cane, blocking the blow expertly. Before Thanatos could respond to the sudden speed that the old man was displaying, the cane's tip had been shoved into his belly, knocking him back a pace.

Goldstein grimaced as his body threatened to betray him. He had a lifetime of experience in battle, however, and he intended to use it. He brandished his cane like a club, slamming it down hard against Thanatos' shoulders. Once he caught the younger man on the jaw, drawing blood.

Thanatos cursed under his breath, furious at the turn of events. He reached up with his glowing hand and caught the cane, crushing it to splinters with a flex of his fingers.

"No more weapons for you," he purred. "Lay down and die."

The former Gravedigger did the exact opposite – he drew back the jagged end of his cane and stabbed at Thanatos, driving the weapon forward with both hands.

The wood dug into the villain's side, painfully cutting through skin and muscle. He howled like a stuck dog but the agony seemed to drive him to new levels of violence. He struck out at Goldstein's face with his glowing hand, the demonically powered blow shredding the older man's lower jaw.

Thanatos pounded again and again, growling with each punch. Goldstein fell back against the window, his features increasingly reduced to a bloodied mess.

The old man slid to the floor when the attack ceased, the air whistling through his shattered nose. Thanatos stood over him, panting heavily. Then he reached down and grabbed Goldstein by the ears. He gave a quick twist, ending the former hero's life.

With a cackle, Thanatos knelt and found the ruby that he'd been sent to retrieve. It shined so brightly that he couldn't help but stare at it for a moment.

Sliding it from the dead man's finger, he dropped it into the pocket of his coat. The glow had faded from his hand, the demonic energy having been expended.

Without even a backwards glance at the man he'd just killed, Thanatos turned and strode from the room.

Gravedigger didn't mind the rain. Growing up in Sovereign, she was used to it. In fact, some nights, she found it easier to sleep when there was a tempest brewing. It mirrored the stormy nature of her emotions.

Mitchell was out in the car, parked surreptitiously down the street. He was listening in via short-wave radio, ready to offer assistance if needed.

Gravedigger stood outside her target's house, noting that every room appeared to be dark. It would certainly make her work easier if no one was home so she quickly began her task. She moved around the brownstone, examining all possible entrances. When she found a window that rattled enticingly, she set to work and quickly forced it open.

Crawling inside, she crept for a moment in darkness, letting her eyes adjust to the gloom. She was in a study of some kind and the faintly cloying odor of the air was at once familiar and repulsive. It was a mix of human sweat and opium, both of which she'd become sensitive to during her youth. Though she'd never gone for drugs of any kind – aside from occasional bits of alcohol – the crowd she'd run with had tried to persuade her to visit various opium dens with them.

Goldstein had described the book to her and she half-hoped that Meeks had left it lying around for her to find. Remove the threat he posed with the tome, she reasoned, and then she could take her time dealing with its owner.

Moving slowly through the home, Charity couldn't help but be impressed by its opulence. The throw rugs alone were worth more than her entire wardrobe!

She was surprised to find a woman in the bedroom. The girl was lying nude on her side, her breathing slow and deep. Gravedigger approached her, nudging the woman's foot. The girl grunted but made no move to wake up.

Assuming that the woman was drugged, Gravedigger turned away from her and resumed her search. She found weapons, perverse items designed for sexual use and a treasure trove of jewels, urns and small statues… but she found no sign of The Necronomicon.

As she glanced at a grandfather clock and took note of the fact that she'd been in the house for over an hour, Charity gave a little sigh of annoyance. This was going to be a wasted evening and she was certain that Goldstein would use this opportunity to show that she'd be better off taking his advice in the future.

It was at that exact moment that she noticed something that had escaped her: a small door set into the wall, hidden by the grandfather clock.

Beneath her mask, Charity's lips broke into a grin. She rushed forward, using all of her muscle to shove the massive timekeeping device out of the way. It was definitely a doorway, with a small depression where a hand would go. She inserted her fingers carefully and found a clasp. After squeezing it, the door swung open with a creak, revealing a set of stairs that led to a hidden basement.

The smells that drifted out of the gloom were a mixture of wet earth, burning incense and human sweat. Gravedigger drew one of her swords and crept down the stairs. For the first time, she wished she had a partner in this – if Meeks returned home, he'd easily see that the hidden door had been found. He could lock Charity inside, without hope of escape.

Downstairs, Gravedigger felt along the wall until she found a switch. With a flip, electric bulbs came on, bathing the room in yellow-tinged light.

The floor was bare earth and was damp. There were three pieces of furniture in the room: two folding chairs and a cot covered by a bloodstained sheet. Gravedigger's attention, however, was focused on the room's sole occupant.

A human figure lay huddled on the floor, their face turned towards the wall and covered by their arms. They were nude and from the shape of the slender form, it was obviously female. Charity wondered suddenly if the drugged woman upstairs was intended to eventually join this poor woman down here in the basement.

The woman's back was crisscrossed with scars, some of them relatively fresh. It was obvious that someone had whipped her terribly and as she shivered fearfully in the light, Gravedigger's heart went out to her.

"Don't be afraid," she said, trying to sound as soothing as possible. She sheathed her sword, knowing that its appearance would clash with her intent. "I'm here to help you."

The woman spun about, showing her face for the first time. Charity felt bile rise to the top of her throat and she jerked back in revulsion. Where there should have been eyes was nothing but smooth skin. The nose was nothing more two small slits in the vast landscape of her face and the mouth was wide and filled with sharpened teeth.

Gravedigger reacted on instinct, raising her right hand. She fired a crossbow bolt that struck home in the woman's throat. Blood spurted from the wound but the female merely reached up and snapped off the end of the bolt. She then threw herself at Gravedigger.

Charity felt the woman's bulk slam into her and she barely had time to throw up an arm in defense. She managed to keep the snapping jaws from her face but the woman was surprisingly strong.

A momentary burst of fear rushed through Charity but she quickly silenced it. She had until October 31, 1939. Until then, she was invulnerable.

A terrible pain ripped through her shoulder as the monster stabbed at her with its claw-like nails.

Thoughts of invulnerability vanished in the haze of combat and Gravedigger renewed her actions, pushing back on the creature's throat. She grabbed hold of the broken crossbow bolt and began to twist it, eliciting a howl of outraged agony from her opponent.

Suddenly freed by the monster's desire to retreat, Gravedigger was able to finally draw her weapons. She unsheathed her sword once more, mentally telling herself to never again put it away unless she was 100% sure it was safe. A curved dagger also appeared in her other hand and she brandished both weapons with obvious skill.

The blind creature hissed like a cat, sniffing the air. Her nasal slits opened and closed as she sucked in air. She seemed to sense that her intended prey was now armed and as such, she crept around Gravedigger, keeping her distance.

"If you can understand me," Gravedigger said, her voice as steely as the blades she wielded, "I don't want to kill you. Surrender and I'll do whatever I can to reverse what's been done to you."

The woman paused, as if digesting Gravedigger's words. Whether or not she truly understood was a moot point as she lunged forward, teeth snapping at the air.

Gravedigger struck expertly – her knife swept up, catching her foe between the breasts, where Gravedigger dug the blade deep. Her sword then came down, decapitating the horrible monster in one fell swoop.

Splattered with blood, Gravedigger stepped back, letting the corpse hit the soft earthen floor. After putting her weapons away, she immediately began looking around the room once more, convinced that this locked room had to be more than a mere prison: the naked woman-thing was a guard of some sort. But what was she protecting?

Kneeling, Charity began poking at the earth. Since there was nothing to be seen above ground, could there be something beneath?

After scooping out several small holes, Gravedigger suddenly yanked her fingers back. Something was *moving* in the dirt! After forcing her hand back into the ground, she felt her fingers close around something slimy and undulating. She yanked it up into the light, revealing a horrible white worm, one end open with a sucking mouth. The creature was as blind as the woman who had guarded it.

Gravedigger shoved it into a pouch on her belt, shivering at the thought of carrying the disgusting creature on her person. It wasn't that she was squeamish about bugs or snakes but something about this thing was unnatural. Further digging showed that there were more of the things, many in various stages of development.

"It's a nursery," she realized with a start. Meeks was cultivating these... *things.*

Realizing that she'd spent too much time on this affair, Gravedigger sprinted up the stairs, not bothering to turn off the lights. Meeks would know she'd been there when he discovered the corpse, regardless. Despite that, she did shove the clock back into place, covering up the doorway.

Then she was out into the night, scurrying off to meet Mitchell. Perhaps Goldstein would recognize this worm that she was carrying and would have advice on how to proceed from here.

Though she was loath to admit it, she was going to need his help on this one.

Chapter V
Death Moves Quickly

Gravedigger and Mitchell knew that something was wrong as soon as they reached the front door. It was partially open, something that Goldstein never would have allowed.

"Miss Grace, let me enter first." Mitchell drew a pearl-handled pistol, his dark face lined with concern.

Charity had changed out of her uniform in the backseat of the car, shoving the weapons and garish clothing into a large bag that was now slung over her shoulder. "I'm not some helpless little girl," she pointed out, setting her bag down and fishing out a curved blade. "You move around back and make sure that no one gets out that way. I'll go through the front."

Mitchell nodded and vanished into the gloom.

Gravedigger swung open the door, slowly creeping inside. It was quiet inside, save for the ticking of the large grandfather clock in the hall. She resisted the urge to call out Goldstein's name, fearful that the old man might not be alone.

She found herself in the study soon enough, having noted that everything appeared to still be in place. If there was theft involved in this, whatever had been taken wasn't immediately evident.

Catching sight of Goldstein's feet, she dropped her weapon and sprinted to his side. He was sitting on the floor, his head tilted downward and his back against the bottom of the window. His face was a dripping mess and Charity fought against the revulsion that suddenly washed over her.

Checking for a pulse, Charity noticed something peculiar. His ruby ring, which had always shined so brightly, was missing.

"How is he?" Mitchell asked. The big man had entered the building and made his own way to the study. When Charity shook her head, he turned away and sighed. "Bloody old fool," he said at last. "I told him that he should always carry a gun but he'd say to me, 'I'm a former Gravedigger, my boy – the day I can't take care of myself is the day I need to die.' I guess he had to be right, didn't he?"

Charity stood up. "His ring is gone."

Mitchell grunted. "Mr. Goldstein told me that it was very old, dating back at least to the Middle Ages. He took it from a black magician in Germany during The Great War."

"Looks like it was the only thing taken so I think whoever did this came here just for that."

"Do you think it was Meeks?" Mitchell asked. He'd listened to Charity's description of the villain's home and remembered how dangerous Goldstein had considered him.

"If it is, then I feel even more terrible. I should have listened to Josef and gone off to kill this guy!"

"You never know how things will go," Mitchell counseled. "I'll be right back." The big man left the room and returned with a sheet. He spread it out on the floor and then lifted Goldstein's corpse, setting it in the center of the sheet.

"We shouldn't move him," Charity pointed out.

"Why not?"

"The police...."

Mitchell looked up at her and smiled, despite the grimness of the situation. "You really think we should call the cops in on this? I imagine they'd ask a few questions about Mr. Goldstein's past... and mine. Not to mention yours. Then you have all the weapons and weird books that are lying around here. Trust me," he added, beginning to wrap his employer's body. "This is what Mr. Goldstein would have wanted."

"What are you going to do with him?"

"I'm going to put him in the car and then I'm going to drive out to the cemetery. I'll bury him in your grave."

Charity nodded. It made sense, though it still seemed wrong not to have a ceremony of some kind for Goldstein. Yes, he'd been annoying, and she couldn't forget that he had shot her and buried her in a coffin – but at his core, he'd been a good man. "I'll come with you."

"You sure?"

"I'm a Gravedigger, right?"

"Yeah, I guess you are." Mitchell stood up, lifting the corpse over his shoulder. Charity noticed that the sheet was already beginning to stain with blood. "Listen, luv, I'll make the same offer to you that I did old Goldstein: I'll work for you and with you, doing the best that I can to assist. But I can't be the man that he was. I don't have his knowledge or his skills."

"That makes two of us." Charity put a hand on Mitchell's arm. "I appreciate that. I'm going to need all the help I can get."

"The house is bought and paid for. Goldstein also told me all the pertinent information about his bank accounts and I know that he put your name on them, as well."

Charity couldn't quite hide her surprise. She hadn't even been sure how much Goldstein liked her, but apparently he'd been making preparations to leave his fortune in her name.

"You're going to do fine, luv," Mitchell said, as if sensing her thoughts. "You and me, we're going to make the next three years count."

"Why?"

"What do you mean?"

"Why did you work for him? Why are you offering to work for me? Were you ever a Gravedigger?"

Mitchell shook his head. Up close, he was a handsome man, Charity realized. "No, can't say that honor ever belonged to me. I met Mr. Goldstein in England. Like you, I didn't have much growing up and I fell in with a bad crowd. One day, we were roughing up a shopkeeper, taking protection money… and then there he was: dressed up like a Halloween spook and swinging a blade like nobody's business. That was one terrifying bloke! He killed my friends and then chased me down an alley. I turned to face him, half hoping that he did kill me. I was sick of living like that. To this day, I'm not sure what he saw in me but whatever it was, he held his killing stroke and told me that I could live, as long as I swore myself to his service."

Charity could tell from the emotion in his voice that Mitchell held a tremendous respect for Josef. It made her feel somewhat guilty for her treatment of the old man, though the memory of him shooting her brought up feelings of confusion.

"Let's go, Mitchell. We have a long night ahead of us – and in the morning, I think we should get started finding out if Meeks is our murderer."

Tʜe Sovereign Museum of Natural History was a sprawling structure. It stood in the heart of the downtown area, and was comprised of twelve interconnected buildings. The Museum housed well over a million specimens, only a relative few of which were on active display. With a scientific staff of over a hundred, the Museum funded nearly four-dozen scientific expeditions each year, sending explorers out all over the globe. The Museum was divided up into numerous displays but the most popular was the ever-present Start of Sovereign Hall, where the origins of the city were examined. To access this, visitors had to stride through the huge entranceway, where they could stare up at a full-size model of a Blue Whale, which hung from the ceiling.

Meeks stood directly under it, staring up at the model, which was built from papier-mâché, iron and basswood. It had been damaged about a year previous but the repairs were such that no one could spot the difference[1].

"I could get into a lot of trouble for this, Mr. Meeks." The security guard said. He was a portly retired police officer named Dinkins. He stood off to the side, shifting his bulk uneasily.

Meeks flashed a smug smile. "I paid you well, didn't I? And if anybody causes any trouble, I'll do the same to them. Money talks in Sovereign – am I right?"

Dinkins laughed, his mood brightening. "Want me to show you where the exhibit hall is?"

"I can find my way. I'll see you on my way out." Meeks waited until Dinkins returned to his desk in the security office. Then he set off down the hall, moving quickly towards his destination. He would, indeed, see Dinkins before he left. He planned to kill the man and pocket the money he'd given him – there couldn't be any loose ends that would tie him to this crime. The worst possible scenario would be for the authorities to arrest him before he had a chance to summon the Old Ones.

Meeks found the urn in a display on ancient Roman artifacts. It definitely didn't look like an object of tremendous occult power. It was cracked in places but remained solid despite its age.

Meeks started to reach out for it when a voice brought him up short. "What the hell do you think you're doing?"

Shocked, Meeks turned quickly and found himself staring into the lovely face of Kelly Emerson. Though many in the city thought of Kelly Emerson as merely "the curator's daughter," she was in fact much more.

---

1 *See Lazarus Gray Volume Two: Die Glocke*

A graduate of Sovereign University, Kelly held doctorates in archaeology and anthropology. Standing nearly six feet tall and possessed of flowing red hair, she looked like a modern Amazon, with enough curves to unsettle even the most ardent of playboys. Her glittering green eyes and full lips had made her one of Sovereign City's most sought-after figures.

To the amusement of gossip columnists everywhere, however, Emerson's heart belonged to local hero Lazarus Gray. Their love affair had titillated the city before Gray's career had torn them apart. Rumor had it that neither had ever truly moved on.

"Arthur Meeks," Kelly said before he could respond. "I know you. You were here for the unveiling of the Scarab collection last month." She strode towards him, her heels clicking on the floor. "Start talking before I call the police!"

"Dinkins let me in...."

"And he's going to get fired," Emerson replied. "Make it quick."

Meeks seethed internally. He'd planned to get away with only killing one unimportant security guard. Emerson, on the other hand, was a prominent figure in the city. Her father would rest at nothing until her murder was solved and the killer behind bars. Beyond that, Emerson's death would bring Lazarus Gray and his Assistance Unlimited team onto the case.

"I can explain," he said, realizing that he had no choice. Within his mind, a wall was sliding into place, signaling a shift from the man he had been born to be – Arthur Meeks – and the man that he now believed himself to be – Thanatos. "I'm fascinated by Roman pottery and I wanted to get a better look at this urn. I was only planning to handle it for a few moments and then put it back."

"You're lying," she replied. "You could have made a sizeable donation to the Museum and my father would have let you look at it. You know that. You were here to steal it, weren't you?"

Thanatos sneered in response and lunged for her, his hands wrapping around Kelly's throat. She staggered under the unexpected assault, her back slamming against the wall. As she fought for breath, the madness in her enemy's eyes struck home.

Thankfully for her, Lazarus Gray had insisted that she learn the art of self-defense. Refusing to give in to the terror that was beginning to mount, she struck back, boxing Thanatos' ears. He cried out but refused to loosen his grip, forcing her to take more drastic measures – she drove her leg up into his crotch, causing his eyes to bulge.

Blessed oxygen flooded her lungs as he backed away, hands over his privates. Knowing that her life was on the line, she took off for the exit, hoping to make it back to her office, where she could call for help.

Thanatos saw her flight and knew that his plan was now at risk. He quickly grabbed a small goblet that was resting next to the urn and threw it. The metal object bounced off Kelly's skull and she slumped to the ground with a pained sigh.

Grabbing the urn, Thanatos was now torn. Should he flee with the object – or kill both her and Dinkins?

His decision was made easier by the lights that suddenly began to come on throughout the museum. Thanatos heard Dinkins' voice, high-pitched and nervous. "I haven't seen her, Mr. Emerson... Are you sure she's still in her office? I thought everyone had gone home."

The curator's response echoed to Meeks' ears. "Yes, I'm sure she's here. There's no need for you to turn on every light in the place! I know this building like the back of my hand!"

Recognizing that Dinkins was trying to alert him to the curator's presence, Thanatos ran from the room, following one of the public halls until he came to an emergency exit. He shoved the door open and hurried to his car. Tossing the urn into the backseat, he started the engine and took off, knowing that his plans were now potentially in ruins.

"I only have one chance," he said to himself. "I have to go into hiding! And Mr. Black's going to have to speed up the timetable!"

Chapter VI
On Wings of Black

Max Davies stepped off the train, adjusting his hat as he did so. He cut a dapper figure, with his handsome face, olive complexion and slightly wavy hair. At thirty-seven years of age, he could easily pass for a man ten years younger.

The son of a crusading newspaper magnate, Max's fortune was ensured from an early age. His good looks combined with his wealth to make him Atlanta's most eligible bachelor for a period, though he had recently given up that status in favor of marriage to the actress Evelyn Gould.

Max flashed a winning smile to a couple of newspaper photo-jocks. They were eagerly taking his picture, shouting questions about what business had brought him back to Sovereign. He moved on without answering, knowing that the gossip columns would be buzzing with guesses of their own, no matter what he said.

What they didn't know was that Max Davies was more than just a philanthropist. He was also the masked vigilante known as The Rook, driven by visions sent from beyond the grave by his dead father. Using those oft-unpredictable bouts of precognition, The Rook had battled monsters both human and demon for well over a decade. During that time, he'd met many important people, some of whom became his close friends.

Just two years prior, he'd visited Sovereign for the first time. The incident had led to a partnership with Assistance Unlimited. Since then, he and Lazarus Gray had maintained a steady contact.

But it wasn't Lazarus Gray who had brought him away from his new bride.

This time, it was Josef Goldstein.

Max had met Goldstein in Germany back in the early 1930s, before the rise of Hitler. Their mutual interest in justice united them and they became fast friends, calling upon each other periodically when the occasion arouse.

Unfortunately, that would never happen again.

Stepping out to the street outside the train station, Max's eyes scanned the rows of cabs waiting for their fares. When he caught sight of Mitchell standing next to Josef's old car, he buttoned his overcoat and headed over, a sad smile on his face.

"You look like marriage is treating you well enough," Mitchell said, shaking Max's hand.

"It's made a new man out of me." Max slid into the backseat of the car when Mitchell opened the door for him. "I'm glad you called me."

"I've spent most of the day making those kinds of calls. Hasn't been easy, mate, I'll tell you that."

"I'm just glad I had business in this part of the country – the train ride only took a couple of hours."

Mitchell got behind the wheel and within seconds, the car was navigating the rain-slicked streets of Sovereign. "Charity is expecting you," the Englishman said.

Max stared out the window, his gaze sweeping all the way to the docks. He could see *The Heart of Fortune* anchored just offshore and he reminded himself to take Evelyn to the gambling vessel sometime. "She doesn't mind me being here?"

"She wants to find the man who killed Mr. Goldstein. She's willing to take any help she can get."

Turning to look at the back of Mitchell's head, Max asked, "Does she know the truth about me?"

Mitchell smiled to himself. It never failed. Every masked vigilante in the world liked to believe that the mask was their true face, while the one they were born with was nothing more than a façade. Sometimes that was true enough but for the most part, it was nothing but a conceit.

"I only told her that you were part of the network of informants that Mr. Goldstein sometimes called upon."

Max nodded, pleased with the response. He closed his eyes, calling up the memories of what he'd seen on the way over. The painful wave of visions had nearly caused him to double over in his railway car, their intensity so strong that it had shocked him.

He had seen the woman that he knew must be Charity, garbed as The Gravedigger. She had been standing amidst a wave of demons, their gnarled bodies dripping with gore. A man dressed all in black was standing nearby, his face hidden beneath a placid ivory mask. Another figure was there, as well, a shadowy male presence that seemed vaguely familiar to Max.

Hovering over all was a vague foreboding, a sense of imminent danger, as if all of Sovereign – if not the world – might be at risk.

———— ❦ ————

C harity was wearing a turtleneck sweater and beige skirt, accompanied by calf-high brown leather boots. She looked beautiful and young, though Max saw in her eyes that she had what his mother would have called 'an old soul'. She was standing in the same study where Josef Goldstein had been murdered, her hands clasped behind her back.

As Max stepped into the room, followed by Mitchell, she moved forward and extended a hand. "Mr. Davies. It's an honor."

Max smiled, accepting the handshake. "Perhaps I can be of assistance?"

"I'm sure you can." Charity offered him a seat and Max noted that she took the one that Josef had preferred. He'd seen that same chair in the old man's German home. "I think that Josef was killed by a man named Arthur Meeks. My first inclination is to go to his home and question him – harshly. I know that he's involved in terrible things. I found... a creature... in his home."

Max leaned forward, amused that Charity had cut immediately to the chase. She wasn't exactly being rude but it was obvious that she wasn't looking to make friends – she needed Max to make her job easier. "So why haven't you?"

"He's not at home," Mitchell said, drawing up a chair and sitting backwards in it. He rested his arms across the back of the chair. "I asked a friend of mine who drives a taxi to go by – there's no sign that he's been back there since last night. Given what's in the papers this morning, I'm not surprised."

Charity reached down into a small magazine holder beside her chair. She passed a copy of *The Sovereign Gazette* to Max, who studied the headline: **CURATOR'S DAUGHTER ATTACKED! MUSEUM RANSACKED!** Then in slightly smaller print: LOCAL BUSINESSMAN WANTED FOR QUESTIONING. The article recounted the stories given by Kelly Emerson and the security guard, identifying Arthur Meeks as the man who had stolen a priceless Roman urn.

"I'm sure he didn't want this to happen," Max said. "All this publicity totally ruins his ability to operate in the open." He looked up at Charity. "You were in his house last night? Did you find the book?"

"I didn't see it."

"Then that makes it very likely that he has it kept in some secret location – probably the same lair he's holed up in now, knowing he can't return home."

"The police have searched his house, too," Charity added. "How come there's no mention of that... thing... that was in his basement?"

Max gave a shrug of his shoulders. "It may not have been there by the time they got there. I've found that most supernatural creatures fade away over time – it's one reason why the whole world doesn't believe in them. There's not enough physical evidence left behind when those things die."

Charity ran a hand through her hair, looking suddenly tired. "How do I find Meeks?"

"You used to be a thief?"

A flush came to Charity's cheeks. "Josef told you that?"

"No. Mitchell did. Is it true?"

"Yes."

"Do you still have any contacts who might be good for sniffing out a missing person?"

"I can't go to them," she said. "Charity Grace is dead, remember?"

"No reason you have to visit them without your new face on."

Charity considered that and nodded. "I know someone."

"Then get started on that." Max set the paper aside and stood up. "Tell them to keep their ear to the ground. Nobody can vanish completely. If Meeks is still in the city, someone knows where."

Charity reached out and grabbed his arm. "Wait. I want you to teach me some things before you leave town. If I'm going to be Gravedigger without Josef, I need to know how to build up a network. I don't have the first clue about –"

"You've already taken the first steps in making your own connections. You have Mitchell. You have me. And now you're about to go recruit someone to serve as your eyes and ears on the street." Max stared hard into her eyes, liking the steel that he saw reflected in them. "You can do this. The Voice chose you for a reason. The minute you start doubting your abilities or the rightness of your mission is when you've already lost everything."

"But what if we don't have time for all this? I was hoping you'd have a suggestion that could help me find Meeks within a few hours."

"I'm not a miracle worker." Max lowered his voice. "I know a thing or two about mystic rituals, though. Whatever he's planning to do with the book is connected both to Josef's ring and to that urn. I'm going to be spending the day piecing together what that could be. Whatever it is, he won't be rushing into it. Screwing up on a black ritual could be catastrophic. With luck, we'll be ready to move on something tonight."

L ess than an hour later, Gravedigger was jumping from one rooftop to another. The overcast day seemed to match her mood and as her feet landed in a puddle, she paused, looking out over the city. She was in the Chinatown district and the entire ambience was different from where she had grown up, despite the fact that the areas weren't more than a few miles apart.

Gravedigger peered over the edge of the rooftop. Clouds of smoke drifted up from beneath the manholes below and a few men were riding bicycles through the crowded streets. A dog was barking somewhere and the sounds of a man and woman arguing in Chinese rang out loudly from one of the overcrowded noodle restaurants.

As she looked around for the girl who had brought her here, Charity couldn't stop wondering about Max Davies. There was certainly far more to him than his role as a wealthy businessman and advisor to Josef Goldstein. The way he moved… it was like he was a panther, possessed of a dangerous grace that was both captivating and a little bit frightening.

Beneath her mask, Charity's face broke into a grin. Here she was, musing about the attractiveness of a married man. Still, she wondered at what his story truly was.

Down below, a young Chinese-American girl stepped out from an incense shop. She wore a red and gold Oriental wrap that flattered her figure and accentuated her raven-black hair. In her late twenties, she retained a youthfulness that helped snag appreciative glances from every man she passed.

Gravedigger hurried to the fire escape and sprinted down it, taking the stairs three at a time. She landed in the alleyway just as the girl was

passing by. "Psst!" she whispered, ducking back into the shadows.

The girl paused, staring into the gloom. Just as Gravedigger had known she would, the lovely young woman moved forward, heedless of the danger. "Is someone in there?" she asked, speaking flawless English.

Li Yuchun was very smart but she was possessed of two dangerous traits: insatiable curiosity and fearlessness. Charity had grown to appreciate that in the girl though it had also led them both into trouble on numerous occasions.

"Li... it's me."

Li stopped, her eyes widening. She recognized the voice instantly but it was too impossible to believe. "Charity?"

"Please don't attract attention." Gravedigger moved into view, letting Li stare in shock for a moment before continuing. "It really is me."

"Why are you dressed like that?"

"I figured you'd ask 'why aren't you dead?'"

"That, too."

"It's a long story."

Li nodded. "So start telling me!" she exclaimed, moving closer. Rather than showing any kind of anger or fear, she was not only embracing the sudden return of her friend but genuinely excited.

Charity gave a quick summary of recent events, starting with how she broke into Goldstein's home. When she got to the part about waking up in her own grave, summoned back by a voice from beyond, Li looked a bit dubious but didn't interrupt. She then sketched out the history of the Gravediggers as best she knew it and finished by telling her that Goldstein had been murdered.

Li laughed, covering her mouth to keep anyone from overhearing. "You're going to be one of those crime fighters, aren't you? Like Doc Daye or The Rook!"

"Sort of. I don't think they're fighting to save their soul, though."

"You really believe that? How do you know Goldstein didn't hypnotize you or something?"

"I woke up in a box."

"So he buried you underground. Still doesn't mean you died."

"Trust me. If you'd been there, you'd believe it, too."

Li crossed her arms over her chest. "So why are you here? Are you going to kill me so I don't tell anyone?"

"No!" Gravedigger replied. "Don't even play like that."

"Have you killed anyone yet?"

"Well… yes."

"I knew it! I've heard stories about a woman with a sword. You killed those two brothers, didn't you? The ones that they think were involved in the little girl's disappearance."

"That was me," Gravedigger admitted. "That's in the past, though. I need your help."

"With what?"

"Did you read about that Arthur Meeks character? The one who broke into the museum last night and attacked the curator's daughter?"

"Yes. I've met him before – he would sometimes come to visit old Bingwen in his shop. The few times I was in there when he arrived, he flirted with me a bit and then Bingwen would push me out of the shop so they could talk in private."

"Well, I think he's the same man who killed Josef. And given that Bingwen is known for selling occult items, it doesn't surprise me that Meeks knows him."

"Is there some sort of black magic stuff involved here?" Li asked, skepticism lacing her words. "I know that Bingwen is into that stuff… though he's got his fingers in opium, too. He used to funnel money for The Ten Fingers." Li knew that her friend was aware of The Ten Fingers, an Oriental crime cartel that was run by the infamous Warlike Manchu.

"Yes. Meeks has gone into hiding and I need to find him. You know a lot of people… could you ask around? See if anybody has seen him or heard anything?"

"Of course I'll help you! I'll start with Bingwen. He's just down the block."

"Be careful. Meeks is dangerous."

Li shrugged. Her fearlessness was evident. "What do I get for helping?"

"What do you mean? You want money?"

"Pshaw! I have money. There are plenty of men who give me presents." Li grinned. "I mean will I get to help out more often?"

"You'd want to?"

"It sounds exciting!"

Gravedigger wondered if Josef had gained any informants this way – because of their innate nature as daredevils. Still, it wouldn't hurt to have a network of aides to help her over the next few years. She had Mitchell already and it looked like she'd be able to call on Max for information… so why not add a femme fatale like Li to the mix?

"C'mon," Li prodded. "Say yes. You know you want to!"

"Do a good job on this… and we'll go from there."

"You're such a tease!" Li exclaimed, laughing.

Gravedigger turned and hurried back up the fire escape. "Get to work."

"Wait!" Li called after her. "How will I contact you?"

Gravedigger didn't answer until she was back on the rooftop. She leaned over the edge and tossed down a business card. Li snatched it out of the air and studied it. An embossed scythe was at the top of the card and below it was an address. Li recognized the street – Gibson Avenue – as it was just a few blocks over from Robeson Avenue, the home of Assistance Unlimited's headquarters.

Looking up, she wasn't surprised at all that Charity was gone.

Tucking the card between her breasts, Li adjusted her bodice and hurried out of the alleyway. She walked straight to Bingwen's shop, which featured no name on the placard out front – there was simply a Chinese dragon painted on its surface. That was enough, since everyone in Chinatown knew the old man with the long white beard and one blind eye.

Barely able to contain her glee, the pretty young Asian American entered the shop. She was eager to join the dangerous world that Gravedigger was offering her and she had no regrets as the door shut behind her.

⊶∞⊷

Gravedigger hoped that she wasn't making a mistake. She had spied on Li as the girl had approached Bingwen's establishment. She loved the other woman like a sister but Li's refusal to bow down before common sense was an open invitation to danger.

A shuffling sound made Gravedigger pause. Perched as she was atop a rooftop, there should be no one up here with her… but that noise distinctly sounded like someone in padded shoes stealthily moving behind her back.

Making sure that her crossbow was ready to be fired, Gravedigger spun about quickly. There was not one man there, but rather three – and all were dressed in identical black attire. She dimly recognized them as ninja – another memory passed on to her by Gravediggers past, she realized. These assassins had been feared throughout history for their murderous zeal.

"I don't suppose you boys would be willing to talk this over, would you?" she asked. Excitement was coursing through her veins and she was ashamed to admit that she was looking forward to the violence.

With a thick Japanese accent, one of the ninja replied, "You have been targeted for death. That is enough."

"That's what I thought." Gravedigger clenched her right hand and a crossbow bolt shot forth, burying itself deep in the ninja's throat. He staggered back but much to Charity's surprise, it wasn't blood that oozed from the wound but something more akin to sawdust.

Realizing that she was once again faced with something beyond the ordinary, Gravedigger unsheathed her sword. It was a move that came at just the right moment for the other two ninja both attacked at once. Her own blade met theirs, the sound seeming very loud to Charity's ears.

She parried another thrust and ducked down to avoid being beheaded. She was functioning on automatic now, allowing her body to fight without her conscious direction.

The ninja with the crossbow bolt in his throat took careful aim and hurled two shuriken. The throwing stars whistled through the air and caught Gravedigger in the thigh of her left leg.

Cursing under her breath, Charity realized that the attack was bound to make her slower – something that she could ill afford.

Eager to end the battle quickly, Gravedigger went on the offensive. She grabbed hold of her sword's hilt with both hands, driving it forward with all her strength. She caught the closest ninja in the belly and then, grunting with the exertion, she yanked up. Her sword sliced him open from belly to throat, spilling dust and dried entrails to the ground.

With a bone-chilling groan, the ninja fell over, whatever awful force that had been powering him no longer in existence.

Gravedigger then threw herself at the next closest ninja, her shoulder striking the undead warrior in the chest. The impact knocked him back and over the edge of the rooftop. He landed in a dusty heap on the street, just in time for a swiftly swerving car to run him over.

The final member of the murderous trio advanced upon her, sword in hand. He whipped it about in an impressive manner, obviously hoping to intimidate her.

Instead, Gravedigger spun toward him, her own sword a blur of motion. The two exchanged parries for nearly a minute before

Gravedigger surprised the man by reaching out with her free hand and grabbing hold of the crossbow bolt. She used it to yank the ninja forward, right onto the end of her upturned blade. She gave it a hard twist and pulled it back, drawing his mummified intestines with it.

There was a moment of regret, where Charity wished that she had kept one of them for questioning. She quickly dismissed the feeling, however. She knew that they were somehow linked to Meeks and she doubted that they would have told her more than that.

After cleaning her blade with a small cloth that she carried just for that purpose, Gravedigger exited the scene. She had to trust Li to do her job – and with any luck, she'd be that much closer to finding her prey.

—⚬⚬⚬—

From the shadows, Mr. Black watched in silence. He had expected the ninja to fail in their mission… indeed, their primary purpose was simply to engage Gravedigger so that he could see her in action. She wasn't the equal of Goldstein at this point but she had a natural ability that surpassed the Jew's.

Knowing that all of his plans were now threatened, the dark messenger of beyond blended into the darkness around him, vanishing completely.

Chapter VII
Roll the Bones

Bingweng stood behind a crowded counter, stroking his long white beard. He said nothing as Li sauntered about, pretending to look at the many odd items on his store's shelves. It wasn't until she turned to look at him, a bright smile on her pretty face, that he spoke up.

"Li Yuchun," he said. "You do me an honor by your presence." He bowed politely.

Clasping her hands behind her back, Li approached the counter. "You're too sweet."

"If you are here inquiring about work, I have none for you."

Li adopted a pouting expression. Though she liked to think of herself as something akin to the Japanese Geisha girls, she was more to the point a prostitute. She did not always service her clients sexually but they certainly paid for her attentions, in some cases simply desiring a beautiful woman to be seen on their premises or with them at social events. "But Mr. Bingweng, surely there's something I can do for you... Would you like me to massage your shoulders? Or I could stand out front for you and bring in customers?"

"That is not necessary. My customers do not visit here because of pretty girls." Bingweng eyed her suspiciously. "You know this... just as you know that I am too old to desire your flesh. So why are you here? What game are you playing, girl?"

Looking defeated, Li sighed and lowered her voice. "You are too wise for me, elder. I should not have even attempted to fool you."

Bingweng grunted. "Tell me what you are after."

"I am looking for a *Laowai* who owes me money," she said confidentially, using the Mandarin word for foreigner. "He came through here not long ago and we spent a pleasant evening together. When he left the next morning, I learned that he had not paid me my wages."

The old man clucked his tongue in disbelief. His lips formed into a frown. "So many Americans are like that," he said, his body language suggesting that he was shifting from a wary stance to one of sympathy. "They come here and take, take, take! They think us fools." Bingweng looked up suddenly. "But why are you here?"

"You know this man and I thought you might know where I could find him. He has come to your shop in the past."

Bingwen stiffened. "His name?"

"It's that man who's in the papers today – Meeks. Arthur Meeks."

"I have not seen him!" he replied hotly. "Now you must go!"

Li blinked in surprise. The old man was known to have a temper but he had shifted so abruptly that she was taken aback. "Did I offend you? If I did…"

"Go!" he bellowed, hurrying around the counter. He literally shoved her towards the door. "And do not come back here again! I know nothing of this man!"

A moment later, Li was on the street outside the shop, hands on hips. She'd certainly struck a nerve, hadn't she?

Suddenly grinning, Li glanced around and then scurried along the side of the shop. She couldn't see past the clutter that blocked the window but she placed her ear against it, hoping that she might hear something useful.

To her glee, she did just that.

Though it was stifled a bit by the wall, she made out Bingwen's voice. He was obviously talking to someone on the phone.

"A *chòu biǎozi* was in here asking about you," the old man said. Li's cheeks reddened at the words he used to describe her – in Mandarin, they meant 'stinking whore.' "She has no contacts with the police, I am sure of that. Her name is Li Yuchun… She claims you hired her and did not pay." There was a moment's pause and Li suspected that Meeks was denying her claims. "I will be there. Five o'clock."

A click told Li all that she needed to know. Meeks wanted a meeting with Bingwen… and all that needed to be done now was to follow the old man when he went to their chosen site.

Li hummed happily to herself as she sauntered away.

───∽∞∞∽───

Shortly after 4:30, Bingwen stepped from his shop and locked the door behind him. A soft drizzle had just ended and the streets were still wet as he began to move away from his home. He kept his head down as he moved and showed no knowledge that someone was following him.

Li had changed her clothing. She now wore a hat with matching blue dress and heels, with enough makeup applied to change her appearance somewhat. In fact, with the hat tilted just so, it was hard to tell that she wasn't Caucasian.

She had thought about visiting Charity and telling her what she'd found out... but in the end, she'd decided against it. She reasoned that it was better to find out more before reporting in.

A thrill went through her, remembering how Charity had looked in her Gravedigger uniform. It was all so terribly exciting, like something out of the pulp magazines that they sold on the newsstands. Li sometimes spent her money on the cheaply printed stories, relishing the lurid covers and exotic settings. She knew that there were real people who led similar lives to those in the stories – Sovereign's own Fortune McCall, Doc Daye and Lazarus Gray being among them – but to actually have a friend of hers turn into a masked vigilante? It was enough to make Li's adventure-loving heart swell.

Bingwen led Li out of Chinatown and into an area of the city known as Hogan's Alley. It was not far from the harbor and was frequented mainly by sailors, many of whom were of the sketchy variety. Li had visited the place before but she hadn't found it very safe and thus usually avoided it. She was a bit surprised that Meeks would choose this part of the city for his hideout but then again, she mused, he *was* trying to lay low... and nobody would be looking for him here.

Bingwen eventually stopped outside an apartment building and studied the row of buttons that were on the switchboard. He buzzed G-8 and after a moment, a voice that Li thought she recognized as Meeks' answered.

"Yes?" Meeks demanded.

"It is I," Bingwen answered.

The door popped open with a electric hiss. "Come on up," Meeks said.

Li rushed forward and grabbed hold of the door before it slammed shut behind the old man. She peeked inside and saw that Bingwen was already moving up the stairs. As quietly as possible, she stepped inside and let the door clang behind her.

It suddenly dawned on her that she should have just stayed out on the street – it was unlikely she would be able to find out anything else from inside the building. She'd confirmed that this was Meeks' new base… Charity would probably be thrilled with that information.

But then she heard the sounds of conversation drifting from above. Creeping over to the stairwell, she leaned over and looked up. She couldn't see anyone above but the old building's walls produced fine echoes that almost made it sound like she was right next to Bingwen and Meeks.

With a huge grin, she realized that Meeks wasn't inviting Bingwen into his apartment – he was talking to him in the hallway!

"What did you tell her? Exactly?"

"Nothing!" Bingwen responded. "I told her to get out of my shop!"

"And you don't think you aroused her suspicions? You should have just shrugged your shoulders and pretended not to care."

Li's grin spread wider. Meeks sounded seriously upset with the old man.

"I thought it best to cut her off before she questioned me further," Bingwen replied. "She is just a nosy whore… do not worry about her!"

"She might go around telling people that you got upset when she asked about me. That's going to start a new round of questions. If you panic when the cops come to see you, what's to stop you from leading them right to me?"

"I would never do that! I have been loyal to you, have I not? I turned away from the Ten Fingers, in favor of you. I've helped you find the occult objects you've needed… and I helped you find this place."

"That's true… and all because you want to receive your just due when I've gotten my power…."

There was a pause before Bingwen agreed, saying that it was only fair payment for all his assistance.

What happened next was somewhat of a mystery to Li, since she couldn't bear witness to it… but its aftermath would be permanently seared into her brain.

There was a flash of light from above, brighter than an exploding light bulb but similar in most ways. Accompanying this was Meeks' raised voice, shouting, "You stupid gook! You're worthless to me now!"

A moment later, a body hurtled over the railing, landing with a thud mere feet away from Li. It was smoking, the flesh having been seared away in a burst of extreme heat. The smell was revolting – a sickly sweet odor that emanated from the old man's body, reminding her of roast duck.

Despite her precarious position, Li couldn't stifle the scream that bubbled up inside her. It exploded in a terrified ejaculation. She tore her eyes away from the corpse, seeing Meeks' head appear over the railing. For a moment, their eyes met and what she saw there was enough to break the spell of fear that had descended upon her.

Li bolted for the door, running out into the streets of Sovereign. She ran as fast as she could, not stopping until she stumbled onto the front steps of 1931 Gibson Avenue.

Gasping, she climbed the front steps and pushed the doorbell. Though she was out of breath and sweating profusely, she still managed to stand up straight and toss her hair when she saw the man who answered the door.

Momentarily forgetting Meeks, Bingwen's death and everything else related to it, she smiled and asked, "Are you Max Davies?!"

———— ఴఴ ————

L i sat back in the cushy chair and sipped her hot tea. She was enjoying the pampering she'd received since her arrival at Gravedigger's home, especially when she'd told about Bingwen's murder. She'd spared no detail, relishing the interest shown by her audience.

Max and Mitchell were standing, both looking very handsome to Li's wandering eye. Charity, dressed in a summery green dress, was seated at her friend's side.

"You're positive it was Meeks?" Max asked. The handsome philanthropist stared at Li with an intensity that brought a flush to the young girl's cheeks. She'd always thought he was handsome, having seen his picture in numerous society columns, but up close, he was breathtaking.

"Positive! He got a good look at me, too."

Charity sighed. "I shouldn't have asked you to do this. Now you're in it deep."

"I had fun!" Li argued, drawing a surprised look from Charity.

"I know you're a daredevil," Charity replied. "But I took advantage of that and sent you into trouble. You could have gotten killed."

"But I didn't."

Mitchell spoke up, his strong British accent seizing control of the moment. "We can't second-guess ourselves, mates. We're a team now, every one of us." To Charity, he said, "Your friends are doing this of their own free will."

Charity looked away. She hadn't really thought of Mitchell as being a friend and that realization shamed her. He'd been very good to her and she certainly needed his counsel.

Max drew up a chair and sat down, resting his elbows on his knees as he leaned forward. "While you were out, Charity, I did some digging around on those objects that Meeks stole. I think I have an idea what he might be up to."

"Let's hear it," Mitchell prodded.

"Both the ring and the urn have histories that suggest they are repositories for sorcerous energies. I think Meeks is going to draw the energy from the both of them and use them to open a gateway."

Li set aside her tea. Her eyes were wide with curiosity. "A gateway to where? Hell?"

Charity barely hid her smirk. Li actually sounded like she was *hoping* for some terrifying reply to come from Max.

"Not quite, but close. According to the information Mitchell and I were able to piece together, Meeks has been collecting rare artifacts and books related to a group of entities known as The Great Old Ones and The Outer Gods. This jibes with what Goldstein told Charity – that Meeks has possession of *The Necronomicon*. I think that Meeks is going to attempt to summon one or more of them to Sovereign."

"Hasn't he ever read *Faust?*" Mitchell asked. "Deals with the devil never work out well."

"That never seems to stop men like Meeks," Max countered.

Charity drummed her fingers on the armrest of her chair. "Okay. So, it's like Josef said… I need to kill him before he can do that." She looked at Max with challenge in her eyes, as if she expected him to try to talk her out of her plan. To her surprise, he nodded in agreement."

"We need to move quickly… before he vanishes again."

Charity stood up. "He may already be gone."

"I doubt it. If he's preparing a major ritual like this, it's not like he can just throw his items into a bag and do it somewhere else. It takes time to prepare. He might still go on the run but I guarantee you that he hasn't done it yet," Max said.

"I'll go get dressed." Charity headed for the door but stopped when she felt Max's hand on her wrist.

With a lowered voice, he said, "Let me come with you."

"Are you going to help me zip up?" she asked, teasing him.

"That's not what I meant."

"I'll have Mitchell in the car. He can provide backup if I need it." Her eyes searched his own, aware that he was close to revealing... something... to her. Again, she thought about the way he moved, the dangerous flex of his muscles, and she wondered about what he did when he wasn't at board meetings.

"Let's go in the other room," he said.

Charity agreed, looking back at Li. "Stay here until I've dealt with Meeks, okay? I don't want anything happening to you."

Li beamed. "A big house like this, stocked with good looking men? You're going to have to throw me out!"

"**S**o what's the big secret?" Charity asked as Max followed into her room. She stepped behind a changing screen and slid her dress to the floor. Her Gravedigger uniform and weapons were waiting for her and she began to change while Max took a second, obviously deciding how to approach the subject.

"Have you heard of The Rook?"

Charity looked over the top of the screen. He was looking away from her, obviously respecting her modesty by not staring at her silhouette. "Is that you?"

"Well... yes. Josef knew that."

Charity finished dressing in silence, stepping out only after she'd pulled her mask on and adjusted her hood. "So you're just as crazy as I am, playing dress-up and fighting criminals."

"Crazier, probably. I have visions of the future, too." He went on to describe what he'd seen of her own fate – of a wave of gore-covered demons, of a powerful man dressed in black and of a sinister presence, hiding above it all. "I think you're going to need my help."

"I'm the one who has three years to prove herself," she countered. "I don't want you screwing that up."

"You don't redeem your soul by getting points for killing the bad guys," he answered. "You have to save lives... you have to become a better person."

"And kill bad guys."

Max smiled softly. "Okay. And kill bad guys."

Charity buckled her sword around her waist and asked, "Josef never said anything to me about becoming a better person."

"He wanted you to figure that out on your own, just as he did. When I first met him, he was a zealot – he worked 24/7 to accomplish his goals because that clock was always ticking inside his head. But eventually, he started slowing down… enjoying life, making friends. And that's when he cleansed his soul."

"So you're going against what Josef would have done by telling me this?"

"Yes. He and I were friends but we didn't always see eye-to-eye when it came to methods."

Charity nodded. "Thank you."

"You're welcome."

"But remember – you're working *with* me, you're not the captain of this ship. Understand?"

Max shook his head, realizing that while Charity might have heard his words, she hadn't taken them to heart. She was still concerned about getting the "credit" for Meeks' kill. "Whatever you say," he agreed.

"I like your accent."

Mitchell grinned, pouring himself a stiff drink. He looked over at Li and was amused to see that she'd pulled open the neck of her wrap, revealing more of her smooth throat. "Thank you, luv. Can I slip a little of this into your tea? Might spice it up a bit."

"Oh, please!" Li stood up and crossed the room. Mitchell could smell her perfume, its pleasant peachy aroma causing him to clear his throat. Li's knowing smile widened as he poured some of the alcohol into her tea. "Do you think I'm pretty?" she teased.

"I think you know just how pretty you are," Mitchell answered, enjoying the little game that was beginning between them.

"Are you going to ask me to dinner?"

"I'd say things are a bit busy at the moment, wouldn't you?"

"This won't last forever."

"I wish I shared your optimism. This Meeks fellow killed my friend and I'm afraid he might kill Charity… and me… before it's all said and done."

Li's facial expression shifted and for the first time since her breathless arrival, Mitchell saw that the young girl before him had additional depth to her. She wasn't just a party girl – there was a strength to her that was surprisingly strong. She set her tea aside and placed a palm against his chest. "Charity was shot and buried under the ground – and she's still here. And I can tell that your life hasn't been all sunshine and happiness. But you're still here. And neither one of you is going to be killed by a sleazy wannabe-warlock like Arthur Meeks."

Mitchell put his hand over Li's and for a long moment the two of them stared into each other's eyes. The moment was broken when Gravedigger strode into the room.

If Gravedigger noticed that she'd interrupted anything, she didn't make mention of it. "Mitchell, is the car ready?"

"I filled up the tank earlier today – so we're good to go." Mitchell's eyes widened a bit as The Rook entered. He'd wondered if Max was going to share his identity – and apparently he'd decided to not only trust Charity but Li, as well.

The philanthropist turned vigilante wore a long coat over his suit and tie but it was the mask on his face that really caught the eye. It was affixed domino-style over his eyes, extending over the bridge of his nose, where it ended in a bird-like beak. "We should park down the block from Meeks' apartment, just in case he's got someone on lookout."

Mitchell gave him a deadpan smile. "Max, I'm not a rookie at this."

"Sorry – I'm used to working alone."

Gravedigger glanced over at him. "Well, this time you're working as a sidekick."

The Rook started to argue that point, not liking the slight she was giving him. Then he realized that she was tweaking him and he offered a salute instead. "Whatever you say, mon capitan."

Chapter VIII
Thanatos Ascendant!

Arthur Meeks worked quickly. Mr. Black was not present but he couldn't wait any longer. The little chink had seen him clearly enough and she'd probably gone to the police by now. Given his druthers, Meeks would have fled this location but it would have been too difficult under the current conditions. Better to just press on and hope for the best, he mused.

A large pentagram covered the floor of his apartment, drawn in equal parts chalk and salt. In the very center of the occult symbol lay Goldstein's ring, the ancient urn and a slaughtered cat. The feline's entrails had been pulled from its gut and spread out in a carefully arranged display.

Meeks wore a finely tailored black suit and a small porcelain mask. He didn't want to greet his new masters as a mere human – he wanted to be Thanatos, bringer of death!

With an almost sexual excitement coursing through him, Thanatos retrieved the cracked leather-bound Necronomicon. He had marked the pages that he needed and had virtually memorized the dead language that he was about to speak. He set the book open on a pedestal near the slaughtered cat and stood next to it, taking several deep breaths to steady his nerves.

This was it, he realized. The moment that he'd dreamed of for so very long. Even as a child, he'd craved the ability to dominate those around him. At first, he used his money and personality to do so but eventually it wasn't enough… he'd turned to black magic, hoping to find the key that would turn things from mere games to deadly seriousness. He didn't just want to order people around… he wanted to control them body and soul.

Mr. Black had offered him the keys to the world… and all it would

take was unleashing demonic forces upon the rest of humanity. It was a fair price, in Arthur's eyes.

Thanatos closed his eyes, his fingers running across the pages. He began reciting the words, looking at them only when he encountered a particularly difficult passage. With his other hand, he rhythmically knocked against his stomach.

"Enoch illesium C'thulhu! Enoch illesium Shub-Niggurath! Planititan onseetus k'rash!"

The words spilled from his mouth like blood oozing from a wound. Each of them was accompanied by a hard punch of his fist. The blows were strong enough that they would leave terrible bruising... but he felt no pain. His mind was alive with the promised power of the ancients.

He was nearing the end of the ceremony when he heard the whining of space ripping in half. Just in front of him, a hole was forming, small in diameter but growing with each passing second. Energy flooded from this portal, passing through his skin and charging him. A tentacle, dripping with black slime, appeared, touching the edges of the portal. The unholy beasts within the other dimension were aching to be free and Thanatos heard their whisperings melding with his own. He was chanting with the denizens of another realm and the spell gained power with their aid.

His skin darkened and became harder than normal. His lungs burned as his nostrils flared, inhaling the scent of the damned. His tongue swelled to the point of nearly bursting and his penis was so hard that it ached.

On and on his words flew. He was moments away from amazing power... moments away from condemning the world to a living hell.

——————

Gravedigger ran up the steps to Meeks' apartment. Her ears were ringing with the horrible, inhuman chanting that was beginning to echo off the walls. She and The Rook had scarcely vacated Mitchell's car when strange lights had begun to emanate from their quarry's apartment.

"Are we too late?" she had asked as they burst into the building.

Max's silence had spurred her on to greater efforts. He had a grim expression on his face and she knew that his fears mirrored her own – if Meeks gained his power and unleashed those demons... then nothing they could do would be enough to save Sovereign City and the rest of the world from torment.

Gravedigger drew her sword and stood outside the door to the villain's apartment. She took a step back and then raised her foot, slamming it into the barricade. On the second kick, the wood began to splinter and she was able to hack away at it with her weapon.

By the time she and The Rook entered the apartment, wind was whipping all around them, sending every loose piece of paper into the air. She squinted against the bright light emanating from the portal, momentarily taken aback by the inhuman limbs reaching through.

And then her eyes focused on Meeks, in his full guise as Thanatos. He looked bigger than she'd expected, his suit barely containing his bulk. A mask hid his face but the skin surrounding it was dark and crispy-looking, as if he were being cooked alive.

"You focus on Meeks," The Rook shouted in her ear. "I'll close that portal!"

Gravedigger gave a quick nod and approached Thanatos. His head whipped towards her and she could tell from his body language, that he was furious at the interruption. He continued chanting as he raised both hands and channeled eldritch energy in her direction. Gravedigger dove to the floor, avoiding the blasts, which tore a hole in the plaster behind her. She slashed out with her sword, slashing at Meeks' closest leg. The impact of her blade against his flesh reminded her of chopping wood – his skin was incredibly dense.

Yanking her blade free of him, Gravedigger scrambled to her feet just in time to take a powerful fist to her left shoulder. Pain flared throughout her arm and the tingling in her fingertips worried her – she wasn't sure the limb would be effective for the rest of the fight.

Responding by raising her right arm and firing her crossbow bolt, Gravedigger was pleased to see the point of her weapon bury itself in Meeks' eye. Blood and gore shot forth from the wound and Thanatos ceased his chanting, though it seemed to be carried on by the creatures within the portal.

Thanatos hissed, reaching up to grip the bolt with both hands. He yanked it free, emitting a roar as he did so.

"You can't kill me!" he shouted. "I am Death! I am the Destroyer of Worlds! I am Thanatos!"

Gravedigger laughed aloud, a sound that seemed to surprise her just as much as it did her opponent. The tone was mocking, rising up deep from her soul. It was the laughter of not just Charity Grace but of all the Gravediggers whose skills she possessed – they had heard many claim ultimate power and in the end, they had all ended up in the grave.

Gravedigger swept her sword through the air, her one good arm driving it towards Meeks with all the supernatural strength she now owned. The blade sliced deep into the villain's neck, encountered stiff resistance, and then finally carried through.

Thanatos' head flew into the air, bouncing off the wall. It landed at Gravedigger's feet.

A loud noise, like the rushing of an oncoming flood, caused Gravedigger to turn towards the portal.

The Rook was there, stabbing at a set of tentacles that were wrapped around his body. His weapon was a dagger that glowed a bright golden color, its surface adorned by ancient runes. From Max's lips were bubbling a series of words that seemed foreign to Charity's ears – but it was clear that they were somehow forcing the portal to shrink in size.

He turned his head and shouted, "Get out of here! When this portal closes, the energy that's been released is going to blow this place apart!"

Gravedigger watched in horror as the tentacles suddenly raised Max high into the air. The portal was sealing itself back up, as time and space fought to restore the natural order of things. But the pressure that was suddenly being placed on Max's body was going to kill him – his quick screams told Charity that.

Rather than flee as he'd said, she rushed towards the maelstrom, sword raised above her head. She brought it down against the largest of the tentacles, slicing it in two. Max hit the ground hard, grunting in pain.

Gravedigger stood in front of the portal, weapons at the ready… and then the hole shrank so quickly that it vanished from sight. Just as Max had warned, the occult energies that had filled the apartment were now running wild.

There was a bright flash of light, followed by a boom that could be heard and felt throughout all of Sovereign.

And then there was nothing, save for silence… and a huge gaping hole in the ground where once there had been an apartment building.

PART TWO
THE STRANGE HORROR OF
HENDRY HALL

Chapter I
Mortimer Quinn

Sovereign City, 1793

Mortimer Quinn had never been in this region before, nestled as it was in the indent of the eastern shore of the river. It was no more than a day's journey from the small market town of Greensburgh, which in the local vernacular was often called Tarry Town.

Mortimer had stopped in Tarry Town for the night and had inquired the woman who ran the inn as to the origins of the local name. She told him, with great alacrity, that it had been given by the housewives of a nearby county, based upon the propensity of their husbands to waste away their hours in the Greensburgh tavern on market days.

Given the high quality of the spirits that Mortimer had sampled during his own visit to the tavern, he had no doubt that these stories were true. The people of Greensburgh were a friendly sort, though their expression turned guarded when he'd asked for stories about his ultimate destination.

Mortimer put little stock in this. As an insurance investigator, he had traveled far and wide. He knew of the petty rivalries that developed throughout the nation, as towns vied for one resource or another. Sometimes all it took was a single slur issued by a public official to spark off a period of disenchantment between communities that would last for generations.

After failing to get much out of his hosts, Mortimer had finished his drinks, engaged in a couple of out-of-tune bar songs with the locals, and then retired to his quarters.

He rose early in the morning, as was his wont, and bathed silently in the basin set out for his use. There was a floor-length mirror in his room and Mortimer had studied his nude form in its surface, counting the scars that lined his right flank. There were four of them, still fiery looking after all this time. Some five years before, he had gone into the mountains in search of a woman named Mary Owen. He had found her, of course – he always found those he sought – but on the way back, he had accidentally stumbled upon a black bear and her cub. The animal had assaulted him and left him for dead. He'd managed to drag his bleeding form all the way down the side of the mountain and though the scars sometimes terrified the women he took to his bed, he was proud of them. They reflected his tenacious nature, he thought.

Mortimer Quinn was aged thirty-two and had worked in his current capacity on behalf of The New England Insurance House for over ten of those years. He was tall and well formed, with the sort of rangy build that men of extreme activity sometimes have. He was neither as broad nor as handsome as some, but the overall combination of his looks and intelligence were usually enough to catch the eye of a single woman – and more than a few married ones, as well.

Mortimer considered himself an upright person but he hadn't looked at a bible in years and his habit of fornicating with women at every stop had gotten him into trouble on numerous occasions. It wasn't that he liked to leave a trail of broken hearts behind him – he genuinely found women to be wonderful companions and, when the feeling was strong within him, he would do nearly anything to bring a smile to the faces of those he courted. Given how much he had lost on behalf of his job, he thought it a fair trade. He had no stable home and was on the move virtually every day of the year. A small bit of lascivious diversion wasn't so bad in the light of that.

After settling his bill, Mortimer set off. By half past lunch, he had come to a small valley nestled between high hills and despite the fact that he was an experienced traveler, he found himself giving pause to examine his surroundings. It was the epitome of the word peaceful: a small brook glided through it, with just enough of a murmur to encourage Mortimer to set down his pack and rest. The occasional chirp of a bird was the only thing to interrupt the scene and even that only served to increase the dreamlike atmosphere of the place.

This was the area known as Sovereign and its dark influence was known throughout the region. Locals swore that ghouls, demons and criminals populated the place. Stories were sometimes told about how the area had been enchanted by an old Indian Chief, in the days before Diogenes Daye had founded the city. Others held that a German doctor had placed a curse upon the land during the early days of the settlement, causing all who dwelt within it to become infused with the sins of gluttony and violence.

As Mortimer approached the place, he remembered how one man in the tavern had told him that the residents of Sovereign lived strange lives, filled with the sorts of events that most people would regard as mere fairy tales.

Supporting that was the strong inclination towards superstition that many in Sovereign were said to possess. Though none in the tavern would dare tell the tale, Mortimer had previously read about one of the more infamous hauntings in the area - a Hessian soldier, killed in the Revolution, was said to still wander the area at night.

According to local legend, the Hessian had been buried in an unmarked grave in a churchyard. Now he and an ebony horse would ride out from amidst the graves, on a grim hunt for his missing head. It was said that occasionally, the Headless Horseman would ride down those unlucky enough to be caught on the roads with him and decapitate them. Whether the Horseman hoped to somehow use these heads in place of his own, or if he simply lashed out in anger, was unknown.

Mortimer bypassed the mayor's office and instead stepped into the local tavern, which seemed to be a nameless establishment. Despite the fact that it was midday, the tavern had several men within. They were clustered in three small groups, two of which had been engaged in small talk. The third group was playing darts. All conversation and game play ceased, with most heads turning to greet the newcomer.

Mortimer nodded at those closest and ambled to the bar. The fellow behind the oak counter had weather skin, thinning hair and dark eyes. He eyed Mortimer with undisguised curiosity, openly studying the fine clothes and perfectly coifed hair.

"Can I help you, sir?" the barkeep asked, his voice sounding smooth as molasses.

"Your best whiskey, if you please." Mortimer set his traveling sack down on the floor and pulled out a wad of paper money that made the barkeep gasp. Mortimer set down enough money to buy everyone in the tavern a round of drinks, several times over. "My name's Mortimer Quinn. I was hoping that you might answer a few questions for me."

"I'll do my best."

Mortimer studied the amber colored liquid that the barkeep poured into a cup. "Do you own this establishment, Mr--?"

"Hendricks. Jacob Hendricks. The owner is Mr. Gumby, sir. I work here during the daytime and he's here at night." The dollars disappeared into Jacob's pockets and Mortimer knew that Gumby would never hear of them. "If you'd like, I can leave a message for Mr. Gumby on your behalf."

"No, no. I think you'll do just fine." Mortimer downed the alcohol in one swoop and he shook his head as the liquid burned its way down his gullet. "I represent an insurance company looking to get in touch with a relative of a recently deceased client."

Hendricks leaned closer, as did everyone else in the tavern. "Somebody around here has inherited some money?"

"Yes. I'm looking for a gentleman who moved here from Connecticut several years ago. All of our attempts to reach him have failed so the company sent me here to investigate."

Hendricks swallowed hard. "Connecticut? You must mean Mr. Hale, the old school teacher."

"Old? Mr. Hale should be in the prime of life. I'd hardly describe him as old."

"I meant he doesn't live here anymore." Hendricks licked his lips, grabbing a dirty rag that he began to drag across the wooden surface of the bar. Maybe you ought to ask the Mayor. He might know something about where we went."

Mortimer looked around the tavern, noting that no one was looking at him any longer. He tapped the bar thoughtfully, raising his voice. "Anybody else here know Mr. Hale? I'm looking for Samuel Hale."

A kindly looking fellow in a worn jacket cleared his throat. "All of us knew him, Mr. Quinn. But none of us have seen him in nearly a year."

"Did he resign his position as school master?"

An uncomfortable silence descended, broken only by the sounds of Hendricks making himself busy behind the bar. It didn't take any of Mortimer's investigative skills to know that he'd stumbled onto something unusual.

"Hale hasn't been seen in many months," the kindly fellow murmured. "Not since he left the party at Chapman's. There are some who think that the Headless Horseman got him."

Mortimer smiled, making it clear what the thought of the local superstitions. "Thank you for the help, gentlemen. Might one of you point me in the direction of the town boarding house?"

Hendricks looked up again, obviously relieved that the topic of discussion had moved on from the whereabouts of Samuel Hale. "Walk to the end of the main street, take a right. You'll see Miss Dietrich's place. She takes boarders and cooks the best breakfasts in the Hollow."

Mortimer left the tavern and strode through the streets, offering a smile to those he met. They, in turn, greeted him in the way that he'd already come to associate with Sovereign: they were pleasant enough but there was something in their eyes that set him on edge. They viewed him with suspicion and in some cases, this verged on the border of hostility.

"Mind if I walk with you, Mr. Quinn?"

Mortimer stopped and turned. A well-dressed man in his early twenties was approaching. He had been in the tavern, amongst the dart throwers. His blonde hair was swept abruptly to the side and he had a beauty mark drawn on the left side of his face, just above a set of pouty lips. That he was a dandy was beyond repute but Mortimer didn't mind. Some of his best friends in the larger cities were dandies. They made good dining companions and were frequently very astute.

"Of course you may. A guide about town would be more than welcome."

The dandy offered a hand. "The name's Wilmer Grace, Mr. Quinn."

Mortimer smiled as they shook. "Please – call me Mortimer."

"Only if you refer to me as Wilmer."

"Agreed."

The two set off in the general direction of the boarding house but Wilmer took Mortimer by the sleeve and steered him down a side street.

"Thought you might want to get a look at the schoolhouse. It's been mostly empty since Mr. Hale vanished but the children still congregate about it some mornings. It's like they're waiting for their schoolmaster to return."

"What do you think happened to him, Wilmer? You don't really believe that some specter killed him, do you?"

"Do I think it's likely? No, sir, I don't. There are other, more earth-bound explanations that seem to jump to my mind. But you won't hear many others in this town talk about them. It's better to think that the root of all evil is of the supernatural sort. Then you don't have to think ill of your fellow man."

"Your thinking mirrors my own," Mortimer said. "So are you unafraid to tell me your theories on the matter?"

"I fear nothing," Wilmer said with a booming laugh. A few passerby glanced at him with exasperation and recognized that his new companion was not the most popular of citizens. "Samuel Hale was well liked around town. He not only taught at the school but he also tutored many in song. Given that he was a bachelor and a notorious eater, he also spent a lot of time visiting homes in the area. His favorite stop was at the home of Katrina Chapman. Her father is a prominent Dutch farmer and Katrina is considered by many to be the most attractive unwed girl in the whole of Sovereign."

"He was courting her?"

"Yes, along with most of the men in the town. His chief rival for her affections was Irving Van Brunt, a ruffian with a quick wit. They were quite a pair, Samuel and Irving. They couldn't have been any more different if they had tried. But both fancied Katrina and she encouraged their sparring. On the night that Samuel was last seen, there was a large party at the Chapman estate. Everyone was there, including me. Eventually a group of people began exchanging ghostly stories. It's a popular pastime in these parts. Samuel recited some tales from a book on the Salem Witch Trials that he owned. And then Irving told a harrowing story about The Headless Horseman. It greatly unnerved Samuel – everyone could see it. When the schoolmaster left, he was shaking from head to toe with fear."

"And no one saw him again," Mortimer mused. "I take it that Irving left soon after Samuel did?"

"He did. With Samuel out of the way, Irving soon won the uncontested heart of Katrinia."

"I like the way your mind works, Wilmer." Mortimer clasped his hands behind his back as they rounded a corner and came to a stop in front of the old schoolhouse. It was a low building, consisting of one large room, rudely constructed of logs. "After we look around this schoolhouse and I get settled in at the boarding house, I think I'll drop in and ask Mr. Van Brunt a few questions."

"That's not going to be easy," Wilmer said with an enigmatic smile.

"And why's that? Has he moved away?"

What Wilmer said next convinced Mortimer that his companion had developed a fine sense of the dramatic. "Irving Van Brunt is dead. His bride woke up on the day after their wedding to find that her new husband was missing. They found most of him out on the lawn of their home."

"Most of him…?"

Wilmer's eyes twinkled. "He was missing his head."

Chapter II
House of Horrors

March 23, 1937

It looked like something torn straight from a nightmare – an old house that loomed against the moonlit sky. It was a massive pile of ancient stone, fine woodwork and dark shadows. The impression that it gave was that it was almost a living thing, this isolated mansion known locally as Hendry Hall - a living thing that was just waiting to sink its fangs into the bodies of all those unlucky enough to cross its doorway.

The clouds that drifted past the bloated moon looked to be full with rain, which was nothing unusual for Sovereign City. The overcast sky combined with the thin layer of fog and the faint, flickering glow that emanated from the ground-floor windows to enhance the almost supernatural feel of the home.

Li Yuchun stared out at the place and felt a thrill go through her. This place was absolutely terrifying!

She'd expected something unusual from the place, given its reputation, but the truth of it far exceeded the rumors. The contrast of the turrets against the moonlight captivated her and brought an instant smile to her lovely face. She was riveted as a particularly large cloud drifted across the face of the moon, leaving the outline of the Manor in silhouette.

"Two bucks, lady. I tell ya what – if you change your mind right now and want to go back to the city, I'll take ya back for free."

Li turned back to the brutish face of her cabdriver. "Oh, no! I'm going to be staying here. Can you drive me through the gate and up to the door?"

"Sorry," the cabbie answered. "You can't pay me enough to pass through those gates. This whole place is bad luck and everybody knows it! The only folks who are welcome here are members of the Hendry family." He twisted around and studied her features. "No offense, lady, but you don't look like you're a Hendry."

"Distant relation," she said with a cheeky smile.

With a grunt, the cabbie stepped out of the car and began unpacking the two small bags that Li had brought with her.

After paying the driver, Li watched the car quickly pull away. She turned towards the gates, studying the house behind. She wore a long tan-colored dress, heels, and a large hat that she positioned at an angle atop her head.

Her heels sank a bit in the moist earth as she moved towards the house. The wind was stirring the wrought iron gates, causing them to creak with an almost human moan. While many women would have trembled at the sound, Li merely smiled and pressed on.

She thought back to what the cabbie had said – that the bad luck that surrounded Hendry Hall didn't affect members of the family. Given the circumstances that had brought her here, she wasn't too sure of that. Even if it had been, that familial shield wouldn't have protected her – given that she was here under false pretenses.

The entire affair had begun with a newspaper account of Maxwell Hendry's death. The elderly patriarch of the family had passed away in his sleep, leaving behind a small fortune… along with rumors of occult dealings and a very peculiar will.

According to Hendry's lawyer, his estate would be divided up between all of his relatives, no matter how tenuous the connection. Anyone wishing to claim a piece of the pie had to be present at midnight on March 23.

Gravedigger had dispatched Li on this particular errand, having forged papers that Li now carried with her. They showed that one of Maxwell's cousins had fathered a child with a Chinese woman. It wouldn't hold up to extended investigation but it would be good enough to get Li inside the house.

The porte-cochere that covered the steps blocked out the moonlight, leaving Li standing in almost total darkness when she reached the door. Setting down her bags, she reached around blindly until her slim fingers made contact with an iron knocker. The clanging sound echoed loudly. When there was no answer, she repeated the knocking, finally bringing someone to the door.

The fellow who admitted Li was the butler, dressed in a faded jacket and stiff shirt. He wore yellow-stained white gloves and had a long face that reminded Li of a bulldog's.

Li stood in the foyer, waiting for the butler to say something, but he merely stared at her in silence after shutting the door. Refusing to speak first, Li playfully glowered at him.

The stare down ended when an old woman's voice issued from a nearby room. "Who was at the door, Sebastian? Another relative, come to pick at the bones of Maxwell?"

The butler turned as if to say something to the unseen figure but Li beat him to the punch. "I don't care anything about the bones but I sure would like some of the money!" she exclaimed.

The butler's bushy eyebrows shot up and his dour expression deepened.

A figure emerged from the room and Li realized that she had come face-to-face with one of the strangest looking women she'd ever seen. The woman was very tall, well over six feet, and cadaverously thin. Her skin seemed shrunken against her bones, accentuating each one. Her silver hair was piled high atop her head and she wore a scarlet shade of lipstick, which only served to make the paleness of her skin more apparent. When the old woman spoke, only her lips moved, the rest of her face apparently frozen. Li noted that she had a pronounced Adam's apple, as well – an unusual feature for any woman.

"Money, you say?" the old crone asked, emitting a laugh that sounded equal parts bark and cough. She stopped and regarded Li with interest. "And you are--?"

"Li Yuchun. Distant relation."

"I should say so." The woman straightened and offered a leathery hand. "My name is Myrtle Hendry. Maxwell was my cousin."

"Nice to meet you. I brought papers."

"The lawyers can sort through them later," Myrtle said. Her touch on Li's hand was brief but the young girl was surprised by how cold the old woman's fingers were. Turning to the butler, she said, "Take these bags up to one of the guest rooms, Sebastian, while I show Miss Yuchun to the parlor."

Sebastian lifted the bags easily and began ascending the stairs, which creaked with each and every step. The interior of the house was illuminated only a few sparse candles, which threw frightening shadows along the walls.

Myrtle put an arm around Li's shoulders and led her into the living room. A large fireplace was crackling, giving much needed warmth and brightness to the environs. There were three people in the room and Li was glad to see them, as she loved making new acquaintances. She was even happier to see that all three were male.

The first man was in his early fifties and well dressed. He had a roundish face, a thin moustache, and one droopy eyelid. Engaged in a game of solitaire, the man looked up when Li and Myrtle entered. His scowl vanished immediately and he stood up, bowing low. He smiled a bit lasciviously at Li, chuckling when Myrtle introduced them. Named Marlowe Wayne, the man was related to the Hendry's through his grandmother.

A bald man named Nicholas Koepp was the next to say hello to Li. He looked surprisingly young to be so bereft of hair. He greeted Li respectfully though a bit coldly – Li wasn't sure if it originated from her race or from the fact that every newcomer meant that the estate's pie was now being sliced into thinner slices.

The third and final man was by far the most handsome. With dark hair, deep-set eyes and a square jaw, Cedric Hendry was a businessman from Pittsburgh. He held Li's hand and gallantly kissed it.

"Thank you, Miss Yuchun, for bringing a ray of sunshine to this dreary old house," he said.

Myrtle gave an unladylike snort. "Maxwell didn't believe in electricity and refused to have it installed. Whoever ends up with the house will have quite a time retrofitting this place."

Li glanced at her. "Surely Maxwell left the house to someone in particular?"

"If he did, we don't know it yet," the old woman answered. "Maxwell insisted that all his relatives be assembled in one place and then everything would be made clear. His lawyer, Jenkins, is already in Maxwell's old office upstairs, getting ready for tonight's ceremony."

"Any reason why he wanted to do it at midnight? I'm normally getting my beauty sleep at that hour!"

"My cousin was quite the night owl… he used to tell me that most of his important work wasn't even started until The Witching Hour. I suppose in death, he thought it amusing to force us all to keep his schedule."

"I wouldn't worry about it," Cedric said. "You look like you could miss whole weeks of beauty sleep and still be the most attractive woman on the East Coast."

Li stifled the urge to roll her eyes. Instead, she lowered her head and looked embarrassed. "You're much too sweet, Mr. Hendry."

"Please call me Cedric."

Li agreed to do so and then she turned to Myrtle. "Do you think it's possible that I could see my room? I know we have over three hours before the reading of the will but I'd like to powder my nose and maybe catch a quick catnap."

"Of course, my dear."

After a series of polite goodbyes, Li followed Myrtle up a set of rickety stairs. The older woman held a candelabrum in her right hand and it was the only thing that kept Li from losing her footing.

"I don't blame you for wanting to get free of young Cedric," Myrtle said. "He's a bit of a wolfhound – he was even going so far as to flirt with me before you arrived."

Li found that hard to believe but she chose not to pursue it. "I'm really just tired from the ride out. The driver wouldn't even bring me through the gate!"

"There are many rumors about this house," Myrtle agreed. "It makes the locals a bit jumpy."

"Really? I haven't heard any stories," Li fibbed.

"Our family has a history of occult involvement. Have you heard of the Sons Or Daughters of Malfeasance?"

"Um, no."

"There are those who think they were the true founders of Sovereign City. That their worshipping of a dark…something… is the real reason why this region is so steeped in the supernatural."

Myrtle took her on a winding path through a number of dark halls and Li realized that she wasn't sure she'd be able to find her way back downstairs. "So our relatives were part of… the Sons or Daughters?"

"That's what some say." Myrtle stopped next to a large window and pointed out towards the back of the property. Li was surprised to see a large cemetery, located behind an abandoned church. The stained glass windows were now broken and weeds had overgrown the tombstones.

"This property has a lot of history to it. That church there was one of the first erected in Sovereign and the cemetery has many notables buried there. Some of the combatants in the bloodiest local battle of the Revolutionary War are interred there." Myrtle looked at her with eyes that seemed to glow in the candlelight. "The Horseman is reputed to be among those buried in unmarked graves."

Li gasped. Like every child born in Sovereign City, she knew the legend of the Headless Horseman and the way it had inspired a writer named Washington Irving to appropriate the story and, with minor tweaks, turn it into a part of American folklore.

"Don't worry, my dear. I think you're quite safe inside these walls." Myrtle chuckled. "At least you're protected from the threats that originate from without."

Glancing at the older woman, Li asked, "What do you mean?"

"I mean that all of us should be on our guard." Myrtle lowered her voice. "Look at logically… every member of the family who is here at midnight shares in the estate. If something should happen to drive one away… or if a terrible accident should end their life before that hour… then each individual piece of the pie gets that much larger. If all of us were to be removed from the picture, then the entire estate would belong to Maxwell's lawyer, Jenkins."

Li hid her nervous excitement, instead adopting the facial expression that would lead Myrtle to think that she was frightened by these suggestions. "Do you really think we're in danger?"

"Stranger things have happened. In fact, at this time last night, there was a man named David Dinkins here. He was a relative on Maxwell's mother's side… I personally showed him to his room and Sebastian said he was definitely there at just past eleven because his room light was still on. But this morning – no sign of him! Nothing! All of his belongings are still in his room!"

"Did you call the police?"

"Jenkins advised us to wait until after tonight's ceremony." Myrtle smiled coolly. "Otherwise, any investigation might force the delay of the reading of the will. And no one wants that, now do we?"

Li agreed that this seemed to be the wisest course of action. The trek to her room resumed and Myrtle had little else to say, except to point out an interesting portrait or two along the way.

"Here's your room, dear." Myrtle opened the door to a room that was rather nice, if a bit dreary in terms of interior design. A large four-poster bed dominated the room but there was also a writing table, two chairs, a changing screen and a small washbasin, as well as a closet. Li's bags were resting on the floor next to the bed. "I hope you'll find it pleasing."

Not wanting to let on that her own home was less than half this size, Li merely shrugged her shoulders and said, "It'll do… it's only one night, after all."

Myrtle made a clucking sound, as if she were terribly embarrassed by the accommodations. "Have a nice rest, dear. If you wish, come and join us in the parlor at your convenience. Otherwise, I'll have Sebastian fetch you at a quarter to twelve."

Once she was alone, Li went quickly to the smaller of her two bags. From an interior pocket on the bag, she produced a tiny flashlight. Stepping over to the window, Li stared off into the thick woods that lined the back of the property. She flashed her light several times into the gloom, sending a message in code.

Within seconds, a reply came back, a series of flashes that told her that Gravedigger was in position. Li wondered how Gravedigger planned to safeguard her during the reading of the will but she pushed the idea out of her mind. She trusted her friend.

She had just started unpacking her bags when a rapping on the window made her jump. She turned back and saw a fearsome silhouette – the lithe body of a woman, swords and daggers sheathed at her sides.

Li opened the window, allowing Gravedigger to drop to the floor. "How did you get up here so fast? We're on the third floor!"

"I'm fast."

"That's what all the boys used to say."

Gravedigger grunted. "How many people are downstairs?"

"Let's see… There's a strange old woman named Myrtle – who might actually be a man in drag – and then there's a lawyer named Jenkins; a butler named Sebastian; and a trio of other relatives." She named them, making sure to remark on how handsome Cedric was.

"Don't get distracted," Gravedigger warned. "Have you seen anything unusual?"

"You mean besides the spooky house, a guy in drag and the fact that the Headless Horseman is buried outside? Not a thing."

"The Headless Horseman?"

"Yep. Buried outside in the cemetery. Unmarked grave." Li snapped her fingers. "Oh! And according to Myrtle, old Maxwell was involved with an occult group called the Sons or Daughters of Malfeasance."

"You don't remember if they were called the Sons or Daughters?"

"No, that IS their name. Sons or Daughters."

Gravedigger shook her head in amazement. "I might have heard of them… supposedly they could shift their gender, amongst other things." She turned back to the window but stopped when Li touched her arm. "Where are you going?"

"Exploring. I want you to go downstairs and get to know these people. Maxwell Hendry's name was in Goldstein's files, along with a notation that he was a dangerous person. If Josef thought he was worth keeping an eye on, that makes me really curious about what all the mystery surrounding his will is really about."

Li nodded, then added, "Are you okay, though? It's your first time out and about since… the explosion at Meeks'"

Gravedigger pulled away, her voice going icy cold. "I'm fine. Now go do your job, please."

Li watched her friend vanish out the window. After a brief sigh, she did as Charity ordered.

It was time to go to work.

Chapter III
A Legacy of Evil

Cedric grinned when Li stepped back into the parlor. He rose from his seat and moved to join her. "You found your way back! I'm impressed. I got lost twice the first time I tried to navigate my way through this darkened maze!"

Li allowed Cedric to guide her over to the fireplace, where two seats were nestled close together. There was no sign of Myrtle but she noticed that Marlowe was still playing cards while Koepp was wandering around the room, lifting up lamps and other bits of furniture, staring at them as if he were appraising their worth.

Cedric confirmed that by whispering, "Baldy there is here for the money and nothing else. He's a cold one."

"And what are you here for, if not the money?"

"I'd like to reestablish the Hendry name in the business world," he said, settling back into his chair. He crossed his legs and studied Li with obvious interest. "There was a time when you couldn't go more than five feet in Sovereign without seeing the Hendry logo plastered on everything from matchbook covers to billboards. But Maxwell let it all go to seed. The family's wealth is still immense but I want to restore it to prominence, as well."

"You have your own business, don't you?"

"I do. We manufacture refrigerator parts. But I want to go far beyond that." Cedric smiled and Li recognized his type: upwardly mobile, with the view that everyone was just part of the ladder he was climbing. She knew what would happen if she ended up in bed with him – he'd ensure his own pleasure, not hers. And then she'd never hear from him again.

"May I ask what you do?" Cedric pressed.

"I'm a daredevil adventurer in service to a masked vigilante."

Cedric's bark of laughter drew a surprised glance from Koepp and a deep frown from Marlowe. "You are a hoot!" he exclaimed. "Let me guess which one… masked, eh? I bet you work with The Darkling. Am I right?"

"I really can't say," Li answered softly. "I took an oath."

Cedric reached out and patted her leg just above the knee. "A daredevil," he said, shaking his head. "I like that in a woman."

Li stood up, eliciting a look of disappointment from Cedric. "I'll be back," she said. "I'd like to get to know the rest of our family, if I could." Before Cedric could respond, Li had sat herself down across from Marlowe.

The sour-faced man looked up from his game of solitaire. "Only a few more hours," he said.

"Oh, I know!" Li leaned forward, her eyes twinkling. "Are you excited?"

Marlowe tugged at his moustache. "I don't get excited."

"Too bad for your wife."

"Excuse me?" he asked, looking shocked.

Li decided not to pursue her little joke. "Well, I'm thrilled. It's so great to not only be a part of this… but to meet new members of my family!"

"Yes. It is… most interesting."

"Married? Any kids?"

Marlowe harrumphed and put down the card he had been waiting to play. "No and no."

Li nodded. "What are you going to do with your share of the loot?"

"The estate," Marlowe corrected, "Is quite substantial from what I have been told. But seeing it split five ways might reduce it quite a bit. Since I don't have any ideas about Maxwell's exact worth, it's difficult to project my future plans."

Li tapped her chin. "You're lying."

"What? How dare you--!"

"I just mean that you strike me as a very careful, methodical person. Heck, you've been contemplating where to put that one card since I first arrived! And you just said you're not the excitable type… so you wouldn't go to something like this without having fully thought out all the angles."

Marlowe said nothing for a moment. When he did speak, his tone had softened somewhat and he seemed to view her through new eyes. "For a woman, you're very clever. Yes, I have plans for my part of the fortune. Over the years, I've become quite the gambler. It's my one vice and I like to study the odds long and hard before I place my bet. Sometimes I win… and sometimes I lose. Unfortunately, I've had more of the latter of late."

"You'd pay off some debts, you mean?"

"Yes. And then I'd translate what I had left into even greater wealth!" Marlowe confidentially lowered his voice. "I know of a sure thing, you see."

Li looked impressed. Inside, she was anything but. So far, she knew that Cedric wanted to become a famous business leader and Marlowe needed a quick influx of cash to handle his gambling debts. That meant one or both might be willing to bump off the competition… but there was no indication that they had or would.

Li excused herself from the conversation without much effort, since Marlowe was keen to get back to his game. The last man in the room was Koepp, who had by this time moved over to an antique vase that rested on a pedestal just inside the doorway.

"Is that worth much?"

Koepp didn't bother looking in her direction. "Why do you ask? Planning to steal it?"

Li's acting skills weren't quite good enough to hide her anger. "I wouldn't want to horn in on your action. You've been casing the place for hours!"

Koepp turned, a smug look on his face. His hairless skull shone in the firelight. "I happen to be an art appraiser."

"I thought you were just money hungry."

"No. That would describe the rest of you, I would think." Koepp leaned closer. "Where I come from, people like you knew their place. And it wasn't in the house."

"What do you mean?" Li asked, though she knew very well what he was implying.

"I mean that all families have a chink or a nigger in the woodpile but usually they stay out in the servants' quarters."

What happened next was such a blur that neither Cedric nor Marlowe truly witnessed it. Li's fist shot forward, slamming into Koepp's nose. The bald man fell back, knocking the vase to the floor, where it shattered into a dozen ceramic shards. Blood streamed from Koepp's wounded proboscis and he cupped it with his hands.

"You little whore!" he shouted. He drew his own hand back,

intending to slap her across the face, but Cedric caught his elbow and held it firm.

"That's enough!" Cedric shouted. Glaring at Marlowe, he added, "I don't know what you said to provoke her but I have no doubt that you were a cad. Apologize."

"Never! Unhand me!"

Cedric drew even closer and his expression became one of tremendous threat. "I'd think about that if I were you."

Koepp withered under the force of the other man's presence. In a low voice, he said, "I apologize for offending you, Miss Yuchun."

Li was rubbing her injured knuckles but she managed to nod her head in acceptance.

Cedric shoved Koepp away, adding, "Maybe you should wait in your room until the lawyer calls for us."

Koepp exited the room, still holding his bleeding nose. The look he shot Li was one that promised vengeance.

"You'd better stay close to me," Cedric warned. "I wouldn't be surprised if he tries to frighten you again. May I ask what he said--?"

"I'd rather not get into it."

"Of course." Cedric kindly led her back to the seat next to the fireplace. "There's a wonderfully stocked bar in the corner. Can I get you something?"

Li's smile returned. Her estimation of Cedric had gone up slightly since his gallant response so she didn't see how a drink could hurt. "I'd love one. Thank you."

——— ⟡ ———

Gravedigger felt like she was at home, wandering through the overgrown cemetery. In just a few months, she'd killed more than her fair share of criminals... already, her name was becoming a common one on the lips of the underworld's major figures. Unlike Doc Daye or Lazarus Gray, she wasn't going to throw the various mob bosses into jail... she was putting them six feet under.

Of course, it had almost been the other way around when Meeks' apartment had exploded. She and The Rook had been thrown nearly half a block by the force of the portal's closing. When Charity had woken up, her uniform had been in tatters and her left arm had been broken in a half dozen places.

Max had been even worse, bleeding from a number of shrapnel-induced wounds. The police and fire department were both arriving and she'd been able to drag him to a nearby alleyway, where she had waited for Mitchell to pick them both up.

The authorities were uncertain as to the cause of the explosion but in the end, they didn't care to pursue the matter. To them, all that mattered was that Meeks was dead. The museum had been upset about the loss of its treasure, of course, but all in all, it seemed to all be resolved.

Gravedigger's recovery had been rapid – far more than it should have been. She had done all she could to help Max but in the end, he had returned to Atlanta to recuperate.

The experience had unnerved Li more than it had Charity. She and Mitchell both thought that Charity should take some time off – that she was moving so quickly that they feared she might still be in shock.

They didn't understand, though. She had no time to waste – the clock was ticking, every day bringing her closer to Judgment.

Something had tickled in the back of her brain when she'd first seen this cemetery and she knew that it was important to investigate it. Li would be fine, she reasoned – the girl could certainly maintain her composure no matter what happened.

In the center of the graveyard was a gnarled oak tree, one that immediately caught her interest. The branches leaned downward, as if they were anxious to seize any unwary soul that ventured too close. The base of the tree was home to a massive hole that seemed to lead into the labyrinthine root system. Gravedigger paused near it and stared into the stygian blackness beneath the tree… Something was *wrong* here but she didn't know for certain what it was.

The sky illuminated for a moment as a jagged arc of lightning cut across it. Gravedigger realized then what was bothering her about the hole and the roots that formed a canopy around it – the entire area seemed to be pulsing… no, *breathing*, she thought.

A jumble of thoughts passed through her mind, then. About Maxwell's links to the occult, to what Li had told her about the Headless Horseman and about things she'd read in Josef's library. Since his death, she'd made a point of reading through everything he'd left behind… and there were several references to the Horseman legend in Sovereign.

Some said that the headless killer was no mere specter. They said that he did the bidding of some higher power – frequently thought to be the devil, of course, but not necessarily. Whoever summoned him needed to first perform a blood sacrifice, which would then give him control over the Horseman.

Gravedigger looked back at Hendry Hall, which stood, angry and frightening, in the distance. Mortimer Quinn, who had spent some time in Sovereign in the late 18th century, had written the book that dealt with the Horseman legend most significantly. He did mention a cult that had lurked in Sovereign around that time but he hadn't named them... Could they have been the Sons or Daughters of Malfeasance?

It was less than an hour before the reading of the will... and Gravedigger felt certain that something terrible was going to happen. She took one step towards the house when she became aware of movement to her left.

Spinning around, Gravedigger took an impact directly to the forehead. She fell back, the world suddenly going black. She had been so wrapped up in thought that she'd missed the signs of danger... and now, she realized, there would be no second chance.

A figure stood over her, a heavy log held in their strong hands. Myrtle looked back at the tree and then turned back to the masked woman at her feet.

"Not much longer," she hissed. "It's almost time for the Horseman to ride once more."

—— ∞∞∞ ——

Charity woke up with her arms and legs tightly bound to a chair. She was inside a small room, sparsely furnished. There were several bookcases filled with ancient tomes and a painting of Maxwell Hendry that dominated the nearest wall. There was one door that led out of the room and she could hear voices on the other side – including Li's. The words were muffled enough that she couldn't understand what they were saying.

Fumbling about with her fingers, she hoped to reach one of her many weapons – but they were all missing.

Movement from behind her made her pause.

Myrtle moved into view, looking very mannish in slacks and a gossamer blouse. She looked into Gravedigger's face, which was still hidden by her mask. "Please tell me who you are."

"Where are my weapons?"

Myrtle gestured to the farthest bookshelf. Sitting on top of it was

Charity's arsenal. "You were very well armed. Expecting trouble, were we?"

"I like to be prepared."

"Always a good idea." Myrtle pulled up a chair and sat down in it backwards, so that her arms crossed over the back of the seat. "Again: who are you?"

"I'm called Gravedigger."

"The vigilante? I've heard of you." Myrtle clucked her tongue. "I pictured you... differently. Taller. More dangerous. Masculine."

"Sorry I disappointed you." Gravedigger tilted her head and her voice took on a curious note. "So why did you fake your death?"

Myrtle looked surprised. "What do you mean?"

"You're one of *them*, right? The Sons *or* Daughters? You can shift your gender from one to the other – but not very well, from the looks of it."

Myrtle stood up, looking angry. Her face shifted, becoming even less feminine. The skin of her face became wrinkled, hanging loosely around the jowls. Her breasts, barely there to begin with, took on a different shape, becoming like those of an old flabby man. "You're a little bitch," Maxwell Hendry hissed.

"Takes one to know one."

Maxwell glanced towards the door. "I'm getting old... death is just around the corner, unless I can barter for more years. And yes, I'm one of the Sons or Daughters of Malfeasance. My ancestors founded this city and bathed its ground in the blood of virgins. We had hoped to gain immortality but it didn't come unconditionally. Our life spans were extended but there were so many things we had to do in order to protect our youth... many of my brothers or sisters failed. They died. Now I'm the only one of my generation remaining! And the younglings think me addled... weak! But I'll show them. I'm going to reawaken our warrior and he'll do the hard work for me. He'll make me young again."

Gravedigger sighed, having had the matter settled for her. She'd held out hope that there would be some rational explanation for all this deceit. But it was simply another case of an insane megalomaniac twisting others for their benefit.

"What's going on in the next room?" Charity asked, grateful that Maxwell couldn't see what was going on behind her back. With deft movements, Charity was busily freeing herself of the bonds that held her in place. It was a skill that had been improved by the trace memories of past Gravediggers but she had already been quite adept at small bits of escape artistry. It came in handy during her days as a thief.

"It's almost time for the reading of the will," Maxwell replied. His face and body were shifting again, reverting back into Myrtle's form. "I've performed the ritual to summon the Headless Horseman but in order to bind him fully to my will, I have to sacrifice blood of my blood... my relatives have to die!"

"And then?"

"Then there are things that the Horseman can do to revive my youth, of course!" Myrtle bowed low. "I'm afraid I have to go, dear. I need to be present when the Horseman arrives – otherwise, he'll be free to roam about on his own accord... and trust me, no one wants *that*."

Gravedigger paused in her escape attempt, lest Myrtle see her furtive movements. The gender-swapping villain merely smiled and said, "And now it's time to end your life, I'm afraid." She stepped over to a small vent and removed the small grating. Inside was a nozzle that she directed into the room and activated by a twist of a dial. "Poisonous gas," she explained, chuckling. "You'll be dead within minutes. Enjoy what's left of your life."

Gravedigger watched Myrtle step from the room, carefully locking the door behind her. Taking as quick a breath as she dared, she went back to work, doing her best to slip one of her wrists free. By spreading her arms as far and as hard as she could, she was able to get a bit of laxness in the rope. Her hand slipped loose and within moments, she was free from the chair. Her lungs were in agony now, desperate for more air, but she knew that inhaling at this moment would be deadly.

With spots appearing before her eyes, she staggered towards the dial. She slipped to her knees, fingers outstretched. In seconds, she'd have to take a breath... but even with the dial being closed, would there be enough of the deadly gas left in the air to finish her?

L i adjusted the hem of her skirt, well aware that she was the object of several people's glances. Cedric was seated at her side, still playing the role of gallant defender. The way his eyes kept drifting over her legs belied his noble intentions, however.

Koepp, his nose bandaged and swollen, sat as far from her as possible. His gaze was full of promised menace, though he wisely looked away whenever Cedric turned in his direction.

Marlowe, too, was watching her, though with far less spite or sexual interest. He seemed to be uncertain what to make of her and Li privately wondered if he wasn't still holding out hope that she would be revealed as a fraud so he could pocket more of the estate.

Myrtle and the lawyer were the only ones who didn't seem to share a fascination with Li. They were huddled together at a large oak desk, going over papers. To Li's eyes, Myrtle was merely going through the motions, however. The older woman smiled and looked attentive whenever the lawyer addressed her but the rest of the time, she was casting furtive glances towards the room's two doors. Was she expecting a late arrival? Li wasn't sure.

"How about you and I share a nightcap when all this is over?" Cedric whispered. "I brought a bottle of wine with me to celebrate… and I hate to drink alone."

Li glanced down as Cedric patted her knee. "That's a very nice invitation," she said. "But aren't you counting your chickens a little early? We haven't even heard the will's contents yet. Might be a surprise."

"I think we're done with those," Cedric replied. "From this point forward, it's just a matter of divvying up the loot." He laughed at his own words. "I sound like a gangster, don't I?"

Before Li could answer, she heard a series of heavy footsteps out in the hall. She craned her neck to look at the door, beside which Koepp was sitting. He heard the noises, too, because he stood up, lest the door hit him when it swung open.

The footsteps came to a stop just outside the room and for a moment, everyone suddenly became tense. A steady drip of water could be heard and then a small puddle began to flow beneath the door.

Cedric broke the silence, looking towards Myrtle. "So you *were* expecting someone!"

Myrtle smiled, covering her lips with a pair of bony fingers. "You're very wise, aren't you, my dear? Not quite wise enough, though!"

"I've had enough of this!" Koepp declared. "I don't know what game you're playing but it's time for the will to be read, by god!" Koepp reached out and yanked open the door, revealing a nightmarish figure.

Dressed in battered, mud-stained clothing, it was The Hessian, given hellish new life. There was no head upon his shoulders, just an awful emptiness from which a terrible stench arose. He held a sword in his gloved right hand and his left was clenched into a fist.

Before Koepp could move, The Headless Horseman had swung his blade, driving it through his victim's body with such force that Koepp's feet left the floor. The Horseman tossed the twitching corpse aside without a care and advanced into the room. He raised his sword with both hands and sliced downward, catching Marlowe in the meat of his shoulder. Yanking the blade free, the undead killer then finished off his foe with a stab to the throat.

Li was on her feet now, Cedrick's hands protectively wrapped around her arm. He was tugging her towards the second of the room's doors – the one that led to Gravedigger's death trap. Allowing herself to be pulled with him, Li asked, "Is that what I think it is?"

"If you mean it's something out of a spook story, then yes!" Cedric found his way barred by Myrtle, who seemed strangely unafraid considering the circumstances.

"Get out of the way, you old bat!" Cedric shouted, trying to push past Myrtle. To his surprise, she resisted with tremendous strength.

"Now, now," she cooed. "You don't want to leave before all the fun is to be had! You have to get your just desserts, after all!"

Li pulled away from Cedric as something warm and wet splattered across the back of her dress. She turned and saw that the lawyer was dead, The Horseman having hacked him to pieces. The headless foeman was now turning towards her and Cedric.

While Cedric grappled with the surprisingly strong Myrtle, Li looked around and snatched up a letter opener that had been knocked off the desk. She brandished it like a knife, stabbing at the air in hopes that it would warn away the Horseman.

The Horseman batted away Li's hand with the side of his blade, causing her to cry out in pain. He then snatched her up by the throat, lifting her high into the air. The young Asian American struggled, kicking and scratching, but to no avail. Just before she blacked out, she saw Cedric slam his shoulder into the Horseman's side, causing Li to slip from the killer's grasp. She landed in a heap, grateful once again for Cedric's assistance.

The Headless Horseman slashed at Cedric, his sword nipping the handsome man's face. A jagged cut bled down the side of Cedric's cheek. He wiped at it with the back of his hand and then drove a fist against the Horseman's midsection. The blow, which looked to Li like it would have rocked a prizefighter, appeared to have zero impact on the ghostly Hessian.

Myrtle was cackling now, her form shifting between male and female. Li looked over at her and saw her clapping her hands above her head. "Kill them all! Kill them all!" she chanted, madness gleaming in her eyes.

And then salvation came, wearing a mask and bearing a blade.

The door that Myrtle had been blocking opened suddenly, revealing Gravedigger. Charity didn't hesitate, driving the point of her sword straight through Myrtle's chest. The point of the blade protruded out, pushing a large chunk of the old woman's heart with it.

As Myrtle hit the floor, a look of stunned amazement on her aged face, Gravedigger stepped over her body and taunted the Horseman. "Headless! Why don't you face someone more your speed?"

The Horseman turned from Cedric, allowing the businessman the opportunity to snatch up Li and carry her from the room. Charity was grateful for the man's quick thinking – she didn't want to worry about her friend while battling this monster.

To her surprise, a deep voice rumbled forth from The Horseman. He spoke with a thick German accent and his tone was cruel. "You have slain the wizard who awakened me."

Gravedigger crouched in a battle stance, holding her sword above her head. "Does this mean you're going to drop your weapon and thank me?"

"Thank you?" the Hessian whispered. "Yes, for that, I will give thanks. You have freed me."

Remembering what Myrtle/Maxwell had said about the Horseman being unleashed without anyone to control him, Charity felt a trickle of fear run down her spine. Facing a talking swordsman who was bereft of a head was strange enough but the quality of his voice was even more unnerving – it was a dark sound, full of hate and fury.

With astonishing speed, the Horseman sprang towards her, his weapon slicing through the air. Gravedigger caught his blow with her own blade and the two of them remained fixed for a moment, each pushing back with all their strength.

Gravedigger broke the tie by spinning away from her foe, allowing his momentum to carry him forward. Now behind him, Gravedigger stabbed her sword into his spine, giving an extra twist with her wrists.

The Horseman, apparently immune to pain, twisted and caught her on the side of the jaw with a gloved fist. The impact was enough to stun Charity and she staggered away in confusion. She was only dimly aware that he was advancing upon her once more but her instincts were such that she raised her hand and fired her mini-crossbow without even realizing it. The bolt caught his wrist as he began to raise it, pinning his limb against the wall.

As her foe yanked his wrist free, leaving behind a trail of gristle, Gravedigger shook her head in hopes of clearing it. She tossed aside her sword, choosing to instead draw two smaller knives. With a cry of rage, she threw herself at the Horseman, wrapping her legs around his torso. She raised both hands high and began slamming them down repeatedly into the Horseman's shoulders. Black, oil-like fluid oozed from the wounds and the Horseman staggered under the assault, though he did not cry out as a normal man would.

Jumping off of him, Gravedigger scrambled away. She was panting now, the exertion of their battle belying how quickly all this had occurred.

"Death, blood and deception," The Headless Horseman said. "Those were the words that best described my human existence. But do you know what was worse than the pain of living? The despair of being resurrected and controlled, like a puppet on strings! Again and again, I was brought back... each time, sent to dispose of those who threatened my masters."

"Did Samuel Hale threaten someone?" Gravedigger asked, remembering the name of the man for whom Mortimer Quinn had been searching.

"He was too smart for his own good," The Horseman warned. "When he was invited to take part in the activities of the Sons or Daughters, he refused. Thus, he had to die. That was a bloody time in Sovereign and I do remember it well."

Sensing that she'd struck a nerve of some sort, triggering some sort of memory that was giving The Horseman pause, she continued to press. "What about Mortimer Quinn? You weren't able to kill him, were you? That means you can be beaten."

The Horseman grew still, as if contemplating the past. "Quinn," he whispered. "How I hate that name." He suddenly reached out and grabbed Gravedigger by the arm. "Why do you taunt me so?" he demanded.

"What happened between the two of you?" she asked, curious despite herself. Quinn's book told of his travels and recounted the legends, adding details that no one had ever heard before... but nowhere did he claim to have personally met the monster.

The Horseman said nothing but a wave of anger rose from him, washing over her like a tidal wave. In its wake, she saw images, she heard snippets of conversation… and she *knew*.

Chapter IV
Mortimer's Trial

Mortimer had searched the school for clues, feeling strangely ill at ease. The empty building had seemed so barren that it had caused a pang of sadness to rise up in the investigator's heart. He attributed this to the gory nature of the crime Wilmer had described.

Wilmer walked him to the boarding house and said farewell at the front door. They agreed to meet for dinner and to walk to the Von Drake farm together.

Mrs. Hendricks had been a stout woman with a nose that seemed altogether too small for her face. She had received Mortimer warmly enough, though with that same distant feeling that Mortimer recognized from others in the town. As she showed him to his room, she'd chattered on in a rambling fashion about how her husband had died three years before, succumbing to a fatal episode of gout.

Mortimer changed clothes before sitting at his desk and writing out a list of what he had so far learned. He placed these papers back into his bag, intending to eventually send it to the home office when he had gotten more details.

He was considering taking a short nap before dinner when a knocking came at the door. He rose and opened it, expecting to see Mrs. Hendricks. Instead, he came face to face with a breathtaking young woman. She was in the full bloom of her beauty, with peaches and cream complexion and a figure that spoke of sensual pleasures. She wore clothing that was a mixture of old-fashioned and modern styles, revealing enough décolletage to draw Mortimer's eyes to her bosom. She wore a solid gold chain around her neck and another on her right wrist.

"Can I help you?" Mortimer asked, forcing his gaze away from her breasts. It was not an easy task.

"I understand that you've been asking questions about Samuel Hale. Is that true?"

Mortimer shifted, being all too familiar with how quickly word traveled in a small town. He noted the concerned expression she wore and something clicked within his mind. "You must be Katrina Von Drake."

Surprise caused her full lips to part. "Yes!"

Mortimer took a step back. "Would you like to come in? My name is Mortimer Quinn"

Katrina hesitated only a moment. She knew that tongues would wag if word got out that she'd been alone in the stranger's quarters but she was not a woman wedded to tradition. This was 1793, after all, and times were changing.

Katrina took the seat that Mortimer had been using at the desk. She clasped her hands together and Mortimer allowed her a moment to compose herself. "I apologize for disturbing you," she said at last. Her voice had a pleasingly lilting quality to it. "Samuel was one of my suitors. He was a very sweet man, with a tremendous capacity for learning. I was very much in awe of him in that regard."

"Your husband was a rival of his," Mortimer said. It wasn't a question but Katrina nodded as if it was.

"Brom used to play the most cruel jokes upon him. I'm ashamed to say that I laughed at more than a few of them. I was attracted to Brom's physical nature but he was so rough compared to Samuel's refined qualities."

"But you married him. You must have found him more than just a handsome face."

"After Samuel vanished, everyone became very afraid of Brom. There were whispers and rumors that he had chased Samuel that night. That they might have had words... or that he might have caused an accident. Brom was the only man who would dare court me then. After awhile... I gave in to his advances." Katrina looked down, continuing to fumble with her hands. "My wedding day was such a happy one. I woke the next day convinced that things had worked out after all. But then I found... I found...."

Mortimer moved towards her, kneeling in front of Katrina as she began to sob. He gallantly handed her a handkerchief from his pocket and consoled her with various words of comfort.

"Why are you here, Katrina? What do you want of me?"

"I want to know what's going on," she said, looking at him with emerald eyes that shone with emotion. "At first I thought that Brom might have hurt Samuel... but then after Brom's death, I wondered if the Headless Horseman might be real after all."

"You don't think Samuel could have killed Brom? Maybe in revenge for whatever happened on the night he disappeared?"

For the first time, Katrina smiled and the radiance she exuded was almost enough to knock Mortimer back on his heels. "Oh, no! That's quite impossible! Samuel abhorred violence and he was skinny as a rail. Brom was easily three times his size and all muscle. Samuel couldn't have hurt Brom if he'd tried with all his might."

"Surely you don't think that some ghost did it."

"I've heard stories about the Horseman my whole life," Katrina said earnestly. "But I always assumed that they were nothing more than that – tales designed to scare little ones. But after Samuel vanished and Brom was killed, I didn't know what else to think."

"In my experience, there's always a rational explanation for things like this. Though the townspeople may not want to hear it, it seems to me that the most likely explanation is that you have a killer amongst you, one who is using the legend of the Headless Horseman for his own benefit."

"I hope you're right, Mr. Quinn, because if that's the case, then the man who did these things can be caught. I'm too young to be a widow but... I am. I want to know what happened to the two men that I loved."

"She knows we're going to speak to her father?"

Mortimer walked alongside Wilmer, hands pushed deep into the pockets of his slacks. After Katrina's visit, Mortimer had dispensed with the notion of a nap. Instead, he had paid a visit to the local blacksmith, who had sold him a saber much like the one Mortimer had used during his stint in the cavalry. He wore it now in a scabbard at his hip. He favored edged weapons to guns, finding them far more worthy of trust. You rarely stabbed someone by accident and as far as he knew, a sword had never jammed at an inconvenient moment. If there was a killer loose in Sovereign City, then Mortimer's questions might drive them into action. It never hurt to be well armed in those cases.

"I told her I planned to speak to all the pertinent individuals in the case. Given that both Icahbod and Brom were at his house that evening, I think I need to speak to him."

Wilmer looked up into the twilight sky. Stars were already in abundance and the sounds of crickets filled the air. He had changed clothes since Mortimer had seen him last and he now wore an outlandish costume: bright blue leggings, knee-high black boots, and a crimson shirt that was fastened with gold buttons. He looked like someone's caricature of a musketeer. "If all your cases are like this, you should have gone into police work. It would have been less dangerous."

"Most of the time, it's not this exciting," Mortimer admitted. He had shared dinner with Wilmer in the boarding house. The roast mutton had been seasoned perfectly and he knew that rumors of Mrs. Hendricks' culinary skills were not overblown.

Wilmer pointed off at a covered bridge leading out of town. It was in the opposite direction from the route that Mortimer had taken upon his arrival. "That's where poor Samuel was done in. All that was found of him was his hat… though there were bits of broken pumpkin alongside it."

"Pumpkin? That's odd."

Wilmer shrugged. "It's a strange thing, indeed."

"On the way back, could you show me the cemetery where the Horseman supposedly rests?"

"Are you putting more stock into our legends now?"

"Hardly. But if there's a killer who fancies the stories, he's likely to haunt the area." Wilmer laughed, leading Mortimer to frown. "This is serious business. I mean to find out what happened to Samuel Hale. Alive or dead, my employers need to know."

"I admire your perseverance but I'm not certain you're going to like whatever answers you find."

Mortimer reached out and touched Wilmer's arm, stopping in the street. Night was falling fast, giving everything a slightly unnatural appearance. Wilmer's pale skin now seemed to glow with a faint blue tinge. "I appreciate the hospitality you've shown me but I begin to wonder why you're doing so."

Wilmer paused and the humor left his face. "I'm sorry, Mortimer. I don't mean to tease you. I've always been an outsider here. My parents moved to Sovereign when I was six years old. My mother and father fell right into place, becoming one of them. But I was always different, always getting into trouble, never finding the right things to say or do. Look at me – do I look like someone Katrina Von Drake would associate with? Or those men in the tavern?"

"You were with a group of them…?"

"Sometimes they buy me drinks when there are no girls around."

Mortimer looked away. "I see. And so you're helping me because I'm an outsider."

"Yes. And the fact is, you interest me. I get the feeling that you'd look into all this even if you weren't being paid to do so. You're like some hero in a fairytale, come to right wrongs and free the people of Sovereign City from the spell they're under."

"I'm no hero."

"We're going to have to disagree," Wilmer prodded. "Now, I'll be your guide and your friend, but you'll have to accept that sometimes I'm a fool."

Mortimer grinned. "Something else we'll have to disagree on, I think. You may be many things, Wilmer, but you're never a fool, I'd wager."

The two men resumed their trek though their conversation was less free than before. When they came within view of the Von Drake estate, Mortimer put a hand to stop Wilmer.

The farm was ablaze, the main house and the largest of the barns both sending thick plumes of smoke into the air. Mortimer broke into a run, quickly leaving the slower Wilmer in his dust. He reached the front door quickly, noting that it had been shattered. It lay half open now, chunks of wood upon the ground. He pulled off his jacket and quickly tied it around his head so that it hung over his nose and mouth.

Stepping inside was like moving into a lit oven. Expensive curtains and tapestries were like kindling now and Mortimer cautiously moved further inside, calling out Katrina's name. A section of ceiling collapsed to his right and Mortimer began to feel his lungs filling with smoke. He wouldn't be able to stay in this place for long but he also didn't want to leave with the Von Drakes possibly inside.

A figure emerged from the flames and for a moment Mortimer thought it might be Katrina's father, for the silhouette was distinctly male, though something about it was not quite right.

Mortimer realized what was wrong with the image a second before the figure came fully into view: the figure wore a Hessian uniform, complete with heavy winter jacket, but it lacked a head. Where a skull should have been was nothing but air, though a foul wound on the entity's neck left no doubt as to the authenticity of what Mortimer was seeing.

The Headless Horseman raised the sword he held in his right hand and Mortimer quickly unsheathed his own, barely getting it out in time to parry a thrust that would have decapitated him.

There, in the midst of the raging fires, Mortimer did battle with a creature straight out of a nightmare. The smoke was clogging his lungs but Mortimer pressed on, doing his best to not only stay alive but to drive back his attacker. As another section of the ceiling collapsed, Mortimer whirled about and jumped over a fallen beam. He ran to the door, knowing that if the Horseman didn't kill him first, then the smoke and fire surely would.

His feet were in the doorway when he felt a strong hand grip him about the collar, yanking him back inside. He twisted his head around to see the Horseman's sword raised high. The edge of the blade gleamed in the firelight and then it descended, leaving behind it nothing but pain and darkness.

This is not a decision entered into lightly. It is a tremendous gesture of faith that are you are about to receive.

The Voice had sounded impossibly loud, filling every available space in Mortimer's head. All around him was darkness, so complete that he could see nothing of his surroundings.

You will have three years in which to redeem your soul. Find those who are unfit for the world of mortals and destroy them: man or demon, the enemy of the innocent is now your enemy. You will put them into their graves and shovel upon them the dirt that symbolizes their eviction from this plane of existence.

On this day in 1796, you will be called back to this place and you will be judged for a final time. If your soul has been made pure, you will find your reward. If your soul is still tainted black... Your suffering will never know an end.

Do you accept these terms? Do you want to live?

Mortimer said nothing for a moment, his mind struggling to conceive of what was being offered. He remembered facing The Headless

Horseman – and of the monster's blade falling upon him. Had he died? Was this the Afterlife?

A sense of desperation settled over him. There were so many things he still wanted to do – so many places to go. This couldn't be the end!

Before he even knew it, he was screaming at the top of his lungs, "Yes! I accept!"

So be it, replied The Voice.

Chapter V
Endings... And Beginnings

Gravedigger jerked away from the Horseman, the images of the past fading as quickly as they had come. Mortimer Quinn had been a Gravedigger! The truth of that was almost overwhelming... It confirmed the existence of The Voice, of Josef's stated history about the continual nature of the role.

And it implied that Josef was not the only one to successfully redeem his soul, for Mortimer Quinn had written his book in 1800, four years after his spiritual deadline.

"Katrina's father was a member of The Sons or Daughters," The Horseman said. "I was dispatched to deal with his enemies... first Hale, then Brom. Finally, he sent me against his own daughter, who had turned against him."

"But Quinn defeated you."

"Only for a time. I cannot be permanently beaten. Not even death can hold me."

Gravedigger danced forward, wielding her blades expertly. She delivered a series of deep cuts that would have incapacitated any normal man... but the Horseman merely stood his ground.

His response was as quick as lightning. He stabbed at her with his sword and the blade would have pierced her stomach if it hadn't been for a perfectly timed throw, one that sent a lawyer's briefcase hurtling between the Horseman and Gravedigger.

Both combatants turned towards the door, where Li was standing there with a grin on her face. She looked like a little girl who had just won first prize in a contest of some sort.

"Yes!" Li screamed. "I did it!"

"Get out of here!" Charity warned, blocking another swipe of the Horseman's blade.

"That's what I've been trying to tell her!" Cedric said, moving into view. He tugged at Li's arm but was unable to contain her.

"You go!" Li shouted at Cedric. "I have work to do!"

Gravedigger sighed, parrying another thrust. She loved Li but the girl was going to get herself killed one of these days. Still… she had to give her credit for the assist.

The Headless Horseman broke off his assault as Li hefted a chair and tossed it at him. It bounced off his shoulder but the distraction was enough for Gravedigger to take advantage. She raised both her knifes and jumped into the air. Again, she brought the blades down but this time, she went straight for the ruined stump where the Horseman's head had once been. The blades bit deep and jets of the inky-black blood spurted from the wound.

For the first time, the Horseman thrashed about in obvious pain. His ghostly voice quavered and he threw all his weight against Gravedigger, knocking her aside. Then, with both knives still embedded in his body, he turned and ran towards the third-floor window. He crashed through, tumbling out onto the slanted roof and knocking aside shingles as he fell. He catapulted off the edge of the roof and landed beside his steed. The horse was pawing at the ground, smoke drifting from its flared nostrils. It was black as midnight, with glowing red eyes.

The Horseman reached up and yanked Gravedigger's knives from his body, tossing them aside. He then sheathed his sword and climbed into the saddle.

Gravedigger watched him from the window, his dark form vanishing in the night.

"Aren't you going after him?" Li asked.

"To what end? I just figured out how to hurt him… but I still don't have a clue how to stop him." Gravedigger turned from the window and looked around the room. Body parts and blood had painted the scene in shades of horror.

Cedric was standing there, surprisingly calm. Charity wondered if he was in shock. Noticing her stare, he asked, "So… Is anyone going to tell me what the hell just happened?"

Mitchell applied gauze to Charity's wounds, ignoring the way she hissed in pain. "I hate seeing you like this, luv."

"Like what?" she asked, pulling her shirt back into place. She was used to being half-naked in front of Mitchell by now but she tried to maintain modesty, for his sake more than hers.

"Angry at yourself." Mitchell sat back and regarded her. He was wearing a black shirt and a pair of pressed slacks. They were seated together in what passed as a first aid station in their shared home. It was a room that had seen altogether too much use in recent months. "You did the best you could."

Charity brushed a strand of dark hair out of her face. Mitchell was struck again by how beautiful she was. It seemed wrong that she wasn't being wooed by scores of handsome men – instead, she was risking life and limb on a nightly basis. "I screwed up. Again. I only saved one person's life – one! Everybody else died."

"If Max Hendry had succeeded, he'd be young again and he'd have The Headless Horseman at his beck and call. You prevented that."

"And now the Horseman is out there in Sovereign… without anyone to reign him in."

"So you'll figure out a way to stop him." Mitchell reached out and placed a hand on her shoulder. He gave it a paternal squeeze and added, "Fighting bad guys isn't all you need to be doing, though. You're supposed to become a better person, remember? That means making friends, forming a family."

"How am I supposed to do that when everybody close to me is at risk?"

"Maybe that's something you have to figure out." Mitchell stood up and began putting away some of the medical tape and gauze that he'd been using. "Li and Cedric are waiting for you downstairs."

Charity grinned. "I've got to stop collecting helpers. It's starting to get crowded around here – though I guess it's good that Cedric has inherited Hendry Hall."

"Cedric wants to help," Mitchell said.

"He wants to get into Li's knickers," Charity said with a laugh.

Mitchell smiled in return. "I like it when you do that. You should try it more often."

"What are you talking about?"

"Laughing."

Charity rose and stretched her back. She avoided looking Mitchell in the eye as she said, "You're a good friend to me, Mitchell. I know I don't say that often enough. If you hadn't been around after Josef died,

I'm not sure what I would have done with myself."

"I'm glad to be here, luv."

The two of them descended the stairs, arm-in-arm. They found Li and Cedric in the study, enjoying drinks and laughing over some joke that Cedric had just told.

Li looked meaningfully at Cedric before turning her eyes towards Charity. She gave a conspiratorial wink that Charity knew all too well. Charity almost felt sorry for Mr. Hendry – he had no idea what he was getting himself into with this flirtation.

Charity stepped away from Mitchell and crossed her arms over her chest. "Both of you are in?"

"Of course!" Li replied, looking shocked that the question even had to be asked.

Cedric seemed less assured but his response was just as definitive. "I think this world is a lot stranger than I ever suspected… and I want to do my part to make it a little safer."

Charity nodded slowly. She then clasped her hands together in front of her and said, "Then let's do this. Mitchell, dig out the newspaper clippings from the past week."

"Already done," he replied, plucking up a folder off a nearby table. Handing it to Charity, he said, "I've taken the liberty of circling several articles that might be of interest."

Charity opened the collection and noticed that there was a rapist active in Chinatown, a mobster had been gunned down in front of the Deja Hotel and a woman was wanted for questioning by the police, with regards to the poisoning of her husband.

"Lots of people have dug their own graves, from the looks of this," Charity whispered. A slow smile spread across her lips. "It's time to throw on the dirt."

PART THREE
The Ferryman of Death

Chapter I
Charon

The assembled mobsters shifted uncomfortably. Sovereign City's underworld had always been a strange thing, governed frequently by madman who bore silly names or outlandish attire. The Monster, Doctor Satan and The Burning Skull were all figures who had populated meetings like this one but it never got easier to take.

Morris Jones was known to most of his cronies as Dash, so named because he had some of the fleetest feet in Sovereign. It was said that if a job went sour, Dash was probably the only one guaranteed to get off scot free – no one, not Lazarus Gray or Fortune McCall – had ever managed to put his mitts around him.

Dash anxiously chewed on a toothpick, his right foot tapping a staccato beat on the floor. Standing before the group, which easily numbered three dozen of the roughest gangsters in the city, were two figures that looked like they'd stepped right out of one of those cheesy pulp novels that Dash devoured like fried chicken.

One of them was the Headless Horseman, dressed in a set of Revolutionary-era clothes. The Horseman's sword hung at his hip and a gloved hand rested atop the hilt. The fact that the Horseman had no head was terrifying, of course, but Dash thought the smell that drifted from the man's wound was far worse.

The other figure wore a hood and robes. His arms looked emaciated but it was the bits of face that occasionally showed that was truly frightening. His cheeks were sunken and his long beard was scraggly. The deep pits of his eyes shone with madness and his teeth were yellowed and crooked. This was Charon, who was just as frequently known as the Ferryman of Death. Dash knew the origins of the name, having been a voracious reader as a child. In fact, though he'd never admit it to his peers, he knew portions of Virgil's description by heart:

There Charon stands, who rules the dreary coast -
A sordid god: down from his hairy chin
A length of beard descends, uncombed, unclean;
His eyes, like hollow furnaces on fire;
A girdle, foul with grease, binds his obscene attire.

Dash stared at the Horseman, feeling uneasy. It was strange how the guy had no head... It had to be a trick of some kind, but he was damned if he knew how the Horseman pulled it off.

Charon spoke up, interrupting Dash's train of thought. The man had a calm, if somewhat aged, voice. "Gentlemen, thank you for answering my summons. I know that many of you are loyal to The Monster or the other crime lords in the city and that you do not want to offend them. Let me assure you that nothing we discuss tonight should do that."

Dash didn't think that was very likely but he didn't speak up. The Monster, in particular, was a stickler when it came to matters of trust. If he thought you were on the take from another mobster or, heaven forbid, the cops, he'd plug you full of lead and drop you off the pier.

"What I am proposing is that each of you act as a clearinghouse of information on my behalf. I have certain things that I want to keep tabs on – and if you come across anything related to those subjects, you pass them on to me and no one else. In return, I will pay you handsomely."

Dash saw a number of people lean forward with interest. He retained his cool, though. He wasn't getting excited about any deal until he knew what the subjects were – and how much he'd get paid for the info.

"I am interested in anyone selling objects of occult power," Charon continued. "If you hear of something, no matter how ludicrous it sounds, you come to me. If it bears fruit, you will receive a bonus. I am also interested in keeping tabs on the various vigilantes in the city: Lazarus Gray, Fortune McCall, The Dark Gentleman, Doc Daye, Gravedigger, etc. If you hear that they're out of town, you pass it on to me. If you hear that they're adding new members to their ranks, I want to know. It's that simple."

"Whatcha gonna do with that information?" Lefty Malone asked. Lefty had lost his hand during a botched robbery a few years ago.

"I plan to carve out an empire for myself in this city," Charon answered. "But it's not one based upon monetary concerns like most. I want to own men's souls." The ferryman laughed but no one joined in. "Let me worry about such things – for you, it's simply a matter of getting paid."

"What's his story?" Dash asked, finally finding his voice. He gestured towards the Horseman.

"He's exactly what he appears to be – he's the Headless Horseman of legend."

"So if you've got some kinda spook on your side, what do you need us for? Can't you use your magic powers to find out all this stuff?"

"As I said, there is no reason for you to concern yourself with the details." Charon chuckled again, a merciless sound that made many in the room shift uncomfortably.

The meeting ended soon after, with only a few of the other criminals asking for mundane details or clarifications. People could reach Charon by leaving a message at the front desks of any of a half dozen squalid hotels – he had people who would receive them.

Dash stepped out into the chill night air and lit a cigarette. He watched as his fellow crooks scattered to their cars or took off down dark alleyways. He lived not far from here, in a run-down little apartment building. The place housed more rats than people, but Dash still considered it home. So home isn't used twice

He still wasn't sure what to make of Charon's deal. It seemed simple enough but he didn't trust the Ferryman or his Horseman… and anything that led to dealings with Lazarus Gray or the other vigilantes simply wasn't a smart move for a man who liked breathing.

He was deep in thought when he approached his apartment building. He nodded at a pretty young Chink who was standing near the steps. She must be new, he mused, because he didn't recognize her as being one of the usual girls who worked the block. If he hadn't been so low on funds, he would have invited her up to his place, but it had been awhile between jobs and he barely had enough to cover the rent.

Regretfully, he passed her by and went on inside. He unlocked his door and stepped through, his hand reaching out to find the light switch. A strong hand wrapped around his wrist and yanked him close, a sharp blade suddenly pressing hard against his throat.

The door was kicked shut behind him, leaving him in total darkness.

"Who is this?" he hissed in fear. He dropped his cigarette and considered fighting back… but the touch of cold steel against his skin made him pause.

A match was struck and a second later, Mitchell lit a candle. He was facing Dash and he looked particularly menacing in the dim light.

"Don't move," he warned.

Mitchell came towards him and began binding Dash's hands and feet with strong wire. Once Dash was bound, the knife vanished from the criminal's throat.

Mitchell dragged the hobbled man over to a chair and pushed him down into it. Dash could now see whom it was that had held him at knifepoint. It was a dame, one outfitted in a red and black outfit that accentuated her athletic physique. The woman's face was hidden beneath mask and hood.

"I'm Gravedigger," she said, sheathing the curved knife that she had been holding. "Tell me what Charon said to you."

Dash swallowed hard. Gravedigger was the worst of Sovereign's vigilantes – Lazarus Gray or The Dark Gentleman would usually cart you off to jail but this woman was known for gutting her prey. "I don't work for him," he stammered. If he was out in the open, he would have taken off by now, hobbled or not. Nobody could match his speed, he was sure of that.

"Didn't say you did," Gravedigger answered, moving closer. She grabbed a wooden chair and set it in front of Dash. Straddling the chair so that she was leaning over the back, she asked, "Now... what did he say?"

"He just asked us to send word to him if we heard about any black magic stuff being sold in the city... and to keep tabs on the comings and goings of people like you. He said we could drop off the info at a bunch of different hotels, like the Clarion or the Nipper."

"People like me?"

"Yeah, you know... the cloak and dagger crowd."

"Anything else?"

"He just said that he'd pay us for the info... and then he said that he wasn't out to make a bunch of cash for himself. He said he wanted to own people's souls."

"Did you believe him?"

"About what?"

"About not being interested in money."

Dash looked at her like she was nuts. "Of course not! Everybody needs dough! The whole mystic bit is just a gimmick... same with the Horseman. He can't be real."

Gravedigger's hand snatched out, grabbing a handful of Dash's hair and yanking hard. Ignoring his cry of pain, she asked, "The Headless

Horseman was there?"

"Yeah, there was a guy there who was pretending to be him! Even had some trick set up so it looked like he didn't have any head at all... whatever effects he was using stank to high heaven, though!"

Gravedigger and Mitchell exchanged a meaningful look before she released Dash's hair. Mitchell walked to the door and started to step out, pausing only long enough to ask, "Are you going to need me for any of the clean-up?"

"No, thanks. I've got this." Gravedigger waited until he was gone and then she drew a long sword out of its scabbard. The highly polished blade gleamed in the candlelight.

"What are you doing to do?" Dash asked, a bead of sweat running down his forehead. Even as he voiced the question, he felt stupid... What else was she going to do with a sword? He suddenly thought about his mother, dead for nearly twenty years. He remembered the look of disappointment in her eyes when she'd first seen him questioned by the police.

"I thought about letting you go," Gravedigger said. "I thought about recruiting you to be one of my agents, too. But over the course of my research into your background, I came across a young woman named Sarah Truesdale. Do you remember her?"

Dash did, though he didn't say so.

Gravedigger continued, taking his silence as affirmation. "She was seventeen years old and two days away from leaving Sovereign so she could attend college. But you attacked her in her own bedroom, raping her for nearly three hours. Then you got worried that she'd be able to identify you... so you poured bleach into her eyes, blinding her."

"I was just a kid. I was barely twenty, myself! I haven't forced myself on another woman in all those years since then!" Dash felt himself beginning to cry. He wished he could run... he was always running, until now. "I'm nothing but a nickel-and-dime lowlife now! I ain't a rapist!"

"Not anymore, you mean?"

"Right! I felt so bad about that girl that I haven't done anything like it since!"

Gravedigger slowly brought her sword to Dash's throat. "But you did it once and now she's got to live with that for the rest of her life. How is it fair that you get to start over and she doesn't?"

"If you cut my head off," he pleaded, "You're nothing but a murderer!

And that's worse than a rapist!"

"I'm not going to murder you," Gravedigger said, causing Dash to swallow in relief.

"You're not?"

"No. You killed yourself a long time ago. The second you poured bleach into that poor girl's eyes. All I'm doing is shoveling the dirt on your grave."

"No!" Dash screamed, but it was too late. The sword whipped through the air, causing a gust of wind that extinguished the candle.

The room was plunged into darkness.

⁂

Mitchell was waiting behind the wheel when Charity slid into the backseat of their car. She had changed out of her uniform in Dash's apartment, stuffing her gear into an oversized duffel bag. "Where's Li?" she asked.

"She decided to take a cab back to Chinatown. She has a date tonight."

Charity ran a hand through her hair, pursing her lips. "Anybody I know?"

"She didn't say." Mitchell pulled out into traffic, glanced in the rearview mirror. "How do you feel?"

"Fine." Charity glanced out the window and sighed. She could feel Mitchell's gaze upon her. "I don't mind the killing anymore. You get used to it."

"You didn't kill him," Mitchell began but stopped when Charity held up a hand.

"I know. I said that to him, too."

Mitchell nodded and turned his eyes back to the road. "He was trash."

"I'm more concerned with the Horseman. No appearances or murders since that night at Hendry Hall… and now he pops up again, working as a guy's enforcer? Seems strange."

"That's all he ever was – a killer who served others," Mitchell pointed out. "Whether it was for the army or for the Sons or Daughters, he takes orders. It doesn't surprise me that he'd eventually seek out somebody to call the shots."

"At least we know that he's using some of the skuzzier hotels for his pick-up points. I'll have somebody watching the Clarion and the Nipper to see if we can catch one of his goons and then follow them."

"Back to the house?" Mitchell asked, though he knew what the answer would be.

"Let's go by the cemetery," she said, so low that he almost couldn't hear her.

"It's morbid the way you visit your own grave."

"Not as morbid as the fact that I *have* a grave."

"Touché, luv."

The man known as Charon hung his hooded robe in the closet and then moved over to a fully stocked bar. He was in one of the most expensive penthouses in the city, overlooking the heart of downtown. If the goons from the underworld meeting had seen him, not a one of them would have recognized him. Gone was the false beard that he wore in their midst and the removal of makeup gave his face a less gaunt appearance.

Born Randall Nipper, he had once been a minor success on the stage. Unfortunately, a tragic accident involving one of his comely costars had ended up getting him blacklisted. For nearly two years, he'd expended the last of his savings. Suddenly destitute, he'd ended up on Skid Row, where he probably would have died if not for a chance meeting that would change his life.

He had been sitting in an alleyway, a bottle of cheap whiskey clutched between his knees. It was well past three in the morning and a string of police cars had roared past, all headed towards the creepy old Hendry Hall. What had happened up there would never be fully revealed in the papers and it was no concern of Nipper's, regardless.

With his head hanging down, he had heard the familiar clip-clop of hooves on wet pavement. Looking up, he'd seen a horseman and rider at the end of the alley. He'd thought himself hallucinating when his eyes had traveled up the length of the man and seen nothing but empty air where a head should have been.

The Horseman had dropped from the saddle and approached him. Nipper had softly risen to his feet, wondering if he had fallen asleep. Surely this was a nightmare, brought on by one too many fanciful stories told to him as a child.

Nipper had stared at the figure before him and before he knew what he was doing, the words had begun to spill from his lips: "All these, however, were mere terrors of the night, phantoms of the mind that walk in darkness; and though he had seen many spectres in his time, and been more than once beset by Satan in diverse shapes, in his lonely pre-ambulations, yet daylight put an end to all these evils; and he would have passed a pleasant life of it, in despite of the devil and all his works, if his path had not been crossed by a being that causes more perplexity to mortal man than ghosts, goblins, and the whole race of witches put together, and that was - a woman."

It was one of Nipper's favorite passages from Washington's Irving's works – and to his amazement, it seemed to give the Horseman pause.

"Why did you say those words?" the Horseman asked, though he had no mouth with which to speak.

"You look like the Headless Horseman… and those are words from *The Legend of Sleepy Hollow.*"

The Horseman reached out a gloved hand and placed it heavily upon Nipper's shoulder. "You seem like a smart man. You know of this world and its mysteries?"

"What… do you mean?"

"I am free for the first time in decades but I have no knowledge of this place or its customs. And my appearance will make it impossible for me to hide myself. I will need assistance. If you can give it, I will let you live. If not… then I will take out my frustrations upon your flesh." To punctuate his words, the Horseman yanked free his sword and held it to Nipper's throat. The action was so quick that it took Nipper several seconds to realize what had happened.

Nipper blinked in horror, knowing that what he said next would determine whether he lived or died. But despite his sins, Nipper was a consummate actor. He closed his eyes briefly and when they reopened, he sounded confident as he spoke. "I can do all that and more. You tell me what you're after and I'll make sure you get it. All it takes is somebody who knows how to work the system."

The Horseman stood back, removing the sword from Nipper's neck. A thin trickle of blood ran into the collar of the man's shirt but Nipper ignored it.

"So," Nipper said, adjusting his stained and dirty clothing, as if he were a king about to greet his subjects. He knew the importance of acting confident – don't give the audience a chance to believe that you're less than the role demanded. "What do you want, Mr. Headless Horseman?"

"I want... a war. That's the only time that I've felt completely at peace. I want to kill. I want to hear my enemies scream. But most of all... I want to remain free."

Nipper nodded. "Then you need to tell me how and why people are able to contain you. Then we kill everybody who might do so." He smiled. "And if I help you, you help me, right?"

"I would be agreeable to that," the Horseman said.

Nipper was thinking about his first meeting with the Horseman when the undead warrior entered the room. Nipper didn't bother turning around – the stench alone made it clear that his companion was approaching.

"I grow restless," the Horseman stated.

Nipper resisted the urge to sigh. He knew that the Horseman had a short fuse when he was like this. Forcing a smile, the actor slipped easily into his role. He turned to face the Hessian and patted him on the arm. "You want me to have some girls sent up? I'll make sure nobody misses them."

The Horseman backed away and Nipper grew cautious. "You promised me blood and mayhem but all I have seen so far are groups of cowardly blowhards preening before us! I am tired of killing helpless women and whimpering fools. Where is this war? Why have we not struck at the men and women in this city who might actually challenge us? This Doc Daye... or Fortune McCall! Instead, you wear a costume and I hover nearby, like a sword waiting to be unsheathed!"

"I'm working on that. You said you didn't want to go back to being anybody's slave, remember? If we're going to hit this town hard, we have to be smart about it. Charon is a spooky figure and I can use that to keep these goons in line. As for you being unsheathed... How about I set something up for you? It'll be what you want."

"When?"

"Tonight." Wagging a finger at the Horseman's chest, Nipper promised, "You have my word."

Chapter II
Death Rides In Silence

Cedric knelt in front of the fireplace, stirring the dying embers with a poker. Hendry Hall was a chilly place at the best of times but on nights like this, when Sovereign was damp and temperatures fell, the house was a veritable icebox.

Since inheriting the estate, he'd spent a good bit of money making alterations but it was never going to be described as welcoming and Cedric was okay with that.

"This wine is delicious."

Cedric looked over at Li, who was curled up in one of the oversized chairs in the room. She wore nothing but a robe, which gapped open in the front to show the curves of her breasts. In her right hand was a mostly empty glass of red wine.

"Would you like some more?"

"My head's already buzzing."

"Is that a no?"

Li smiled and downed the last of her drink. She then held out the glass. "It's definitely a yes."

Cedric laughed and moved to get her a refill. "So why haven't you told Charity about us?"

"There's no us," she said pointedly. "We're friends."

"We're lovers," he countered.

"That implies some sort of romantic feelings."

"We make love."

"We have sex." Li looked at him with something akin to pity. "I know that men have trouble differentiating between the two but sex and making love are not the same."

Cedric shook his head. "I think it's usually women with that issue."

"Regardless, I don't love you and you don't love me. But Charity has enough things to worry about – if she knew you and I were doing… this… it would only distract her."

Cedric knelt in front of her. He set her wine down on the table next to Li's chair and grasped her hands. He looked very earnest. "I've never known a woman like you, Li! I've had my share of lovers and never did I have feelings beyond the physical for them! But you excite me in ways that they never did!"

"Don't confuse me being really good in bed with being a special kind of woman," Li said. "I think you're being really sweet but I don't believe you if you say you're in love with me. I'm a challenge to you, that's all. If I ever gave you what you're saying you wanted, you'd lose interest." Li leaned close, her expression becoming catlike. "Do you know how I know that?"

"How?"

"Because I'm the same way."

Cedric stood up, an expression of amusement on his face. "You're going to be the death of me."

"But what a way to go, eh?" Li teased.

⸺ ✸ ⸺

Gravedigger stood at her own grave, ignoring the pink-tinged fog that clung to her ankles. The name on the tombstone – Charity Grace – seemed to hover in the air above the mist, as if taunting her. *Someday you'll be here for good,* it promised, *only your soul will be rotting in Hell.*

Charity reached out and traced the letters with her fingertips and then turned away. She spotted Josef's grave and quickly looked away, still feeling guilty for the way she'd treated him.

She'd taken only a few steps when she noticed that she wasn't alone. Standing about twenty feet away from her was a figure that she recognized all too well – Lazarus Gray, leader and founder of Assistance Unlimited.

He was also the employer of Samantha Grace, Charity's half-sister.

His mismatched eyes – one a startling emerald, the other a dull green – stared at her with authority. His athletic physique seemed barely contained by the suit and tie that he wore. Despite her ambivalent feelings for him, Charity had to admit that he cut a dashing figure.

Charity looked around for any sign of Mitchell but he wasn't in his

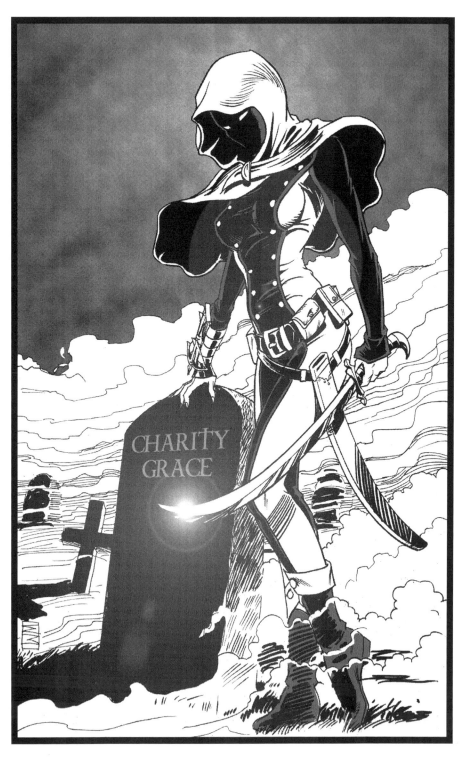

usual spot at the edge of the cemetery – in fact, their car seemed to be gone.

"You and I seem to have something in common," Lazarus said.

"What's that?" she asked, wishing that she hadn't left her weapons in the vehicle.

"We both have a penchant for coming back from the dead."

"I've heard rumors," Charity replied. "But I thought they were a bunch of bunk. Did you really die?"

"Yes and no." Lazarus took a few steps forward but stopped when Charity looked like she might bolt and run. "How about you?"

"I did. A higher power offered me a shot at redemption and I took it."

Lazarus studied her closely. "And now you're killing people. Did you murder Josef Goldstein? You're living in his house."

"What did you do with Mitchell?" she asked, refusing to answer him.

"He's fine. My associates just took him away so that we could talk in private."

"I know Mitchell. He wouldn't have gone quietly."

"He didn't," Lazarus admitted.

"Why are you here?" Charity asked.

"I've heard rumors about The Gravedigger but it took me awhile to figure out if they were true – and once I had done that, who might behind the mask. I had to station informants all around the city before one of them noticed that Goldstein's house was still being used, despite the fact that he died months ago. I wasn't sure if it was connected to Gravedigger or not – but a few days of watching the property led me to you, a dead girl. Suddenly, things began to make a little bit of sense. You killed Goldstein, possibly in cahoots with Mitchell, who turned on his employer. Now the two of you live in his house and have set yourselves up as judge, jury and executioner."

"You're wrong about several things."

"Such as?"

"I didn't kill Josef. He was training me when a nutcase named Arthur Meeks murdered him. The Rook and I teamed up to bring him down."

There was a subtle shift in Gray's expression, so minor that most would have missed it. Charity knew that it was in response to her mention of The Rook – while he didn't trust her, it was obvious that Gray did trust Max Davies.

"So you're a vigilante?"

"If you want to call it that." Charity took a deep breath. "I was serious about dying – and about being given a second chance."

"You're saying that God sent you back to murder criminals?"

"I don't know if it's God. It doesn't matter, really. Josef was a Gravedigger and there have been others before him. I'm the first woman to ever have the mantle and I plan to be one of the ones who survive. I only have three years to do it in."

"What happens after three years?"

"The Voice returns and it judges me. If I've redeemed my soul, then I'm a free – and better – person. If I haven't, then my soul is condemned to Hell."

"I don't think killing people is the way to redeem anyone."

"That's what The Voice told me to do. And I'm not just killing random people – I'm killing people who've dug their own graves. I'm taking scum off the streets."

Lazarus reached into his jacket and Charity tensed. She grew even more still when a pistol appeared in his hand. He pointed it at her and said, "We're going back to Robeson Avenue. I'm going to ascertain whether or not you're sane. If you are… and I've encountered enough strange things in my time to admit that you may be… then I'll offer you a position with my group. We kill from time to time, but only when there's no alternative."

Charity felt an anger rising up within her. There was no turning back after today – even if she managed to defeat Lazarus and escape, he knew where she lived. He was aware of her allies and could reach out to harm them. And he had the bargaining chip of Mitchell's well being, something she couldn't ignore.

On the other hand, she wasn't about to become a prisoner of anyone, especially not her half-sister or her employer.

Charity moved quickly, reaching out with her left hand to smack Gray's gun hand. With the barrel no longer pointing in her direction, she felt better about raising a foot and kicking him hard in the midsection. It was like striking an oak tree and he showed no sign of having been pained.

Lazarus brought his pistol around again and fired, his shot narrowly missing her torso. As she spun away from the blast, she noticed that it wasn't a bullet at all – but rather some sort of specially made tranquilizer dart.

Charity dropped down and spun about, her foot knocking Gray's legs out from under him. He went down but recovered quickly, getting off a second shot from his prone position. This time, Charity performed an acrobatic back flip that once again allowed her to avoid being shot.

Clutching a handful of dirt in her hand, Charity hurled it into Gray's face. The act momentarily blinded him and allowed her to lunge towards him without fear of being caught. She had caught a flash of something sheathed under his coat – a dagger. Realizing that she needed a weapon to even the odds, Charity grabbed hold of the blade and yanked it free. As she did so, the edge of the weapon caught Lazarus under the chin, leaving a tiny cut in its wake. Blood oozed from the wound but Charity felt no regret about its presence – she was the victim here, not the other way around.

Now armed, Charity struck quickly – she slashed her blade across Gray's chest, slicing his tie in two. Another line of blood appeared.

Gray now used his gun as a bludgeoning weapon, clubbing Charity in the shoulder. She winced but refused to fall – instead, she drove the blade into Gray's hip. Yanking it free, she started to strike again but she was distracted by a sharp stinging sensation in her neck.

Staggering back, Charity realized what had happened, even before she reached up to yank the tranquilizer dart from her throat. She turned her head, seeing Gray's "associate" at last. Samantha Grace stood there, looking beautiful in an ankle-length coat, turtleneck sweater and form-fitting skirt. She looked like she'd stepped right off the society page of *The Sovereign Gazette*, with the addition of a pistol, of course.

Charity swayed on her feet. She fell forward into Gray's arms, darkness claiming her.

The Headless Horseman sat atop his steed, hiding in the stygian shadows that cloaked Sovereign. He was positioned outside the home of Inspector Cord, a well-known member of the police department. Cord was on the straight-and-narrow, which put him at odds with many of the more corrupt officials in the city. But the whippet-thin man with the perpetually narrowed eyes was no friend to men like Lazarus Gray, either. He despised vigilantes almost as much as he hated crooks.

Cord stepped out from his house, a cigarette dangling limply from between his tightly clenched lips. He headed towards his car but stopped abruptly when he saw the bodies draped across the hood.

Even with the damage done to them, he recognized them: O'Hara, Gibson and Drake. Three of the best cops on the force, good and decent men who had families.

Cord's shock lasted for only a moment before he reached for his holstered gun. The killer or killers were likely to have fled the scene but if they hadn't....

A sharp blade touched the side of his neck, giving him pause.

"Draw your weapon and die."

Cord couldn't see the figure behind him but he sure as hell could smell him. "Who are you?" he demanded, using the same voice he used on two-bit hoods when he was shaking them down.

"You should avoid Charon," the Horseman replied. "You and your men have been asking too many questions. Now they won't be able to ask anything, ever again."

Charon. Cord's jaw clenched tighter. He might have known it would be one of the city's freaks. "I'm going to see you fry for this," he promised. "You and your buddy Charon."

The Horseman increased the pressure against Cord's throat. "You still taunt me? When death is so close?"

"You don't scare me. Kill me if ya want," Cord said defiantly. "I'd rather die with my chin up then beg."

The Horseman leaned close, remembering the way that he had met Charon... Nipper had proven to be a disappointment. But here he was, again with a man who refused to back down in the face of his own demise. Would Cord have been the better person to ally himself with?

It was too late for that, the Horseman mused.

"I'd like to see you die," he said, his ghostly voice echoing in Cord's ear. "But I have chosen my side in this conflict and Charon has asked me to leave you alive. Do you know why he thinks you are more useful to him in this way?"

"I'd love to hear it – because he doesn't know me very well if he thinks I'm not going to come after him with everything I have after this."

"These men were known for their honesty. The fact that they were all killed while you alone were left alive... do you know what people will think?"

Cord's eyes widened. He knew exactly how this would be perceived – people would think he was now on the take. "You bastards," he hissed.

"My reputation is the one thing I've got."

The Horseman stepped away. "Not anymore."

Cord whipped around, planning to strike back – but there was no one there. Not even a hint of the Horseman remained.

Chapter III
Assistance Unlimited

Charity woke up, her head pounding. She opened her eyes, finding herself in a well-furnished room that was not her own. Even without any other evidence, she could guess where she was: 6196 Robeson Avenue, home of Assistance Unlimited. Housed in a former luxury hotel, the building still retained that old feeling.

Mitchell sat on a second bed in the room, flipping through a battered copy of Bram Stoker's *Dracula*. He tossed it aside when he saw Charity pushing off the mattress. "Sleeping beauty awakens!" he said, smiling broadly.

"Are you okay?" she asked, rubbing her temples.

"I'm fine, luv. My own headache faded after a bit and yours will, too."

"I can't believe they caught us. Josef must be rolling his eyes in heaven."

"We're going to be okay."

"How do you figure that? We're prisoners." Charity looked up at him, annoyed that he was still smiling. "At best, they're going to keep us on a leash. At worst, we're going to jail. I'm going to spend my three years making license plates."

Mitchell swung his feet off the bed, facing her. "If they wanted to turn us over to the police, they could have done so. We were as helpless as babes. The fact that they didn't makes me think that they have other plans – and I don't think they're going to keep us around at all."

"What makes you think that?"

"Well, we just need to make sure they contact The Rook. He'll vouch for us."

"I namedropped him. Doesn't mean they'll forget all the bodies I've left in my wake."

"Max is pretty persuasive and I think he has a good rapport with Lazarus Gray."

Charity stood up and wandered over to a mirror. She looked tired but otherwise unharmed. "I wonder if they're listening to us right now."

"Probably. If I were them, I would be."

"Do you think she knows who I am?"

Mitchell's smile faded and he became more serious. "Probably. I know you didn't meet her during that whole blackmail scheme of your boyfriend's – but I'm sure she knows your name."

Charity sighed. "I'm more afraid of talking to her than I am of facing Lazarus."

"Why?"

"Because a part of me is jealous of her! And now she's going to be superior to me – again. She's a hero, I'm a killer. It's like all my worst nightmares come to life."

"You have nothing to be ashamed of."

Charity laughed coldly. "Oh, please. You mean besides the criminal record and the murders? Not to mention the fact that she's gorgeous and I'm... I'm me."

Mitchell turned her face towards his. "Are you joking? You're absolutely beautiful. And you've done things that you needed to do to survive. You weren't born with a silver spoon in your mouth the way she was."

Charity stared at him, her eyes widening slightly as he leaned closer. His lips parted and she knew what was about to happen though she wasn't certain how she was going to respond.

She was saved from making that decision by a rapping at the door. Charity turned away and asked, "Yes?"

Samantha stepped inside, looking nearly as uncomfortable as Charity felt. It occurred to Charity that she hadn't given any real thought to how Samantha would take this meeting.

"Lazarus wants the two of you to come down to the briefing room," Samantha said. She addressed those words to both Charity and Mitchell but it was Charity alone who received her glance. "I've always wondered what you were like."

"You could have found me," Charity answered, immediately regretting her tone. "Sorry. I shouldn't treat you like the enemy."

"I thought about looking for you," Samantha replied. "But I wasn't sure how big a role you played in the blackmail scheme. And my father refused to talk about you or your mother so... I was scared, I guess. It was bad enough that I learned my father wasn't the perfect figure I'd grown up believing him to be. To then learn that he had another daughter... I wasn't sure I wanted to draw any comparisons between us."

Charity looked stunned. "But you had everything! Why would you be scared of how I turned out? Nothing I accomplished was going to hold a candle to what you've done."

"My life hasn't been all sweetness and light."

Charity stepped towards her, hands clenching into fists. "I don't know how to speak to you," she admitted.

Samantha smiled shyly. Up close, she didn't look nearly as perfect as she seemed in the newspaper photographs. She was gorgeous, yes, but she was very human. "If it makes you feel any better, I don't know, either. But we are related by blood... and from the looks of things, we both have a penchant for getting into trouble. Maybe we should get to know one another."

Charity resisted the urge to respond sarcastically. It was part of her nature to do so when upset but she sensed that Samantha was being sincere... and, deep down inside, she wasn't against the notion of having a family again. She'd been alone for a very long time – she'd started to think of Mitchell, Li and Cedric as a family of sorts but she was hesitant to commit too deeply given how easily any of them could be killed.

"I... I'd like that," she said at last.

Charity was relieved to see that her uniform and weapons were lying on the table when she entered the briefing room. She wanted to grab hold of her sword, desiring its comforting weight in her hands, but she held off.

Lazarus Gray was standing at the head of the table, his handsome face drawn and serious. Seated on either side of him were a glowering young Korean whom she recognized as Eun Jiwon and a man in his forties, with a perfectly tailored suit and a small, well-tended moustache. This was Morgan Watts, a former criminal who had joined the side of the angels thanks to Gray's intervention.

Charity spoke first, wanting to take control of the situation. She knew that Mitchell was at her side and out of the corner of her eye, she saw Samantha taking a seat. "Are you ready to let us go?" she asked.

Morgan grinned at her audacity but her words had the opposite effect on Eun. The Korean's frown deepened and he obviously would have responded if not for a glance from Lazarus.

"We are, actually," Lazarus replied. "But only with certain conditions."

"Like what?"

"Well, The Rook vouched for you, as I'm sure you knew he would. He also corroborated your story about some sort of mystical form empowering you."

Thank you, Max, Charity thought to herself.

Lazarus crossed his arms. "But he and I are in agreement that you're going to get yourself in hot water if you keep murdering criminals. He's found himself the target of law enforcement before and has recently taken steps to curb the number of deaths associated with his investigations. I want you to do the same."

"Take it up with The Voice," Charity responded. "I was told to 'shovel the dirt' onto their graves. The Voice didn't give me much leeway about that."

"Nevertheless, I think you're putting too much emphasis on the killing aspect of what The Voice said. From what I understand, you're also supposed to become a better person. I know from personal experience that it's hard to do that with blood dripping from your hands."

"I second that," Morgan said.

Mitchell cleared his throat. "We can stop killing."

Charity looked at him in shock but Mitchell pressed on.

"But we don't want to feel like you're watching over us like spies or something. You have to trust us, mate."

Lazarus paused and then nodded. "Fair enough. But if I hear that Gravedigger is killing again, I'll come knocking – and this time, I'm not going to go easy on you."

"**W**hat the hell was that about?!" Charity shouted, as soon as they were back in the car. Her equipment was thrown into the back seat, leaving her free to stare down Mitchell.

He started up the car and began driving before he answered. "I lied."

"You lied?"

"That's what I said, luv. I told them what they wanted to hear so they'd let us go free."

Charity shook her head, chuckling. "Lazarus is going to hate us."

"I think we should abandon Josef's house."

"I don't see why...."

"Because they know it's our base!" Mitchell glanced over at her, ignoring the way a driver going past honked his car's horn. It was one thing to see a black man driving a white woman around when it was obvious he was nothing more than a chauffeur – but with the two of them sitting side-by-side in the front seat, the societal boundaries were being blurred and not everyone appreciated that. "We should move into Hendry Hall. Cedric's new to the group and they may not even know he's working with us. Besides, the place is huge – there's more than enough room for all of Josef's books and for us, too."

"I don't know if Cedric would appreciate us moving in."

"Of course he would. He wants to impress Li and that means impressing you."

"Moving to a new house in town isn't going to keep them from finding us."

"It'll slow them down for awhile. And in the meantime, we can plan how to deal with them in the future."

Charity glanced at him. "So were you going to kiss me back there?"

Mitchell smiled. "I don't know what you're talking about."

"Liar. You were definitely going to kiss me."

"Luv, I hate to break this to you – but you're not even my type."

"Oh, really? And what is your type?"

"I like a girl with a creamy cocoa complexion. And a big bosom."

Charity rolled her eyes and laughed. "Ah, I fail in both regards, then."

"Well... your bosom is okay." Charity pinched him. "Ouch!" he said, chuckling.

A silence fell between them but neither seemed to mind. It was good to be with someone who knew all your secrets, Charity realized.

Chapter IV
Endings and Beginnings

Charon stood at the head of the table, cloaked in his hood. Just off to the side and behind him was the Headless Horseman, whose mood seemed somewhat lighter this morning. Nipper knew that the murders would only slake the Horseman's need for violence for a short time, so it was best to make the most of this.

Facing Charon was a fit young man named Morrissey. He was a third-rate goon from the looks of him, with a taste for narcotics and cheap whores. "So I know it's not really big news but do you think you can use it?" he asked, licking his lips nervously. A large cold sore seeped painfully from the corner of his mouth.

"I wanted details about the city's vigilantes," Charon said, each word hissed from between clenched teeth. "But you bring me details about a shipment of drugs."

"I know, I know – but this is a lot of snow, we're talking about. The Ten Fingers are trying to horn in on the Sovereign City action, spreading out from Chinatown and into the rest of town. I figure that a guy like you would want to know about it."

Charon moved around the table, his robes shifting with each step. He put a skeletal hand on Morrissey's shoulder and drew him close. "Tell me again – what time are they arriving?"

"The boat's supposed to come into the harbor at midnight."

"And you're certain that there won't be much in the way of security?"

"Nah. They paid off the cops so they won't be around. And besides the guys on the boat, there's only gonna be two or three guys waitin' to unload the stuff. It's easy for the takin'!"

Charon patted the man's back. "Thank you, my friend, for telling me this. Though it is not the sort of information that I would normally seek out, I will see that you are handsomely rewarded."

"Thanks!" Morrissey gushed. He looked very eager as he asked, "I was thinking that maybe instead of money, I could get a sample of the take...."

"The cocaine, you mean?"

"Yeah! I'd really appreciate some of the snow, if you wouldn't mind...."

"Something can be worked out, my friend. Have no fear." Charon steered him towards the door. "I will be in touch."

When he was gone, Charon turned to the Horseman. "We need to be there tonight. We'll bring some gunmen with us."

The Horseman shifted. "This does not sound like a challenge."

"Not everything has to be." Charon pulled his hood back, revealing his disguised face. "Look – remember the deal," he said hotly. "You get to kill and I get rich."

The Horseman backhanded Charon so hard that the villain flew across the tabletop. He landed on the floor, rising slowly.

"You will not speak to me in such a tone," the Horseman warned. "The next time that you do, I'll kill you. Do you understand?"

"I'm well aware of the true nature of our alliance," Charon replied, wiping away a trail of blood that was leaking from his upper lip. "Forgive me. I'm just anxious to start getting what we both want. If we steal these drugs from The Ten Fingers, they'll want retribution. That will lead to that war you want so badly – but I'm counting on you to protect me and to kill all of them!"

"I will not be stopped by the weapons of this age... bullets, knives, explosives... all are too little to halt my progress."

"Good. 'Cause these boys play for keeps. Now, as I was saying, we'll be there to night with some of our goons. We'll take the drugs and then we'll make a killing on the open market, selling it for less than the Ten Fingers would ever do. It's all profit for us and it'll get us a foothold into the drug running biz. Once we've done that, we'll start buying our own supply."

The Horseman said nothing and Charon took his silence as acceptance of the plan. Personally, Charon was beginning to wonder if there wasn't some way he could rid himself of the unearthly guardian at some point – but not too soon, he cautioned himself. He still needed the Horseman to solidify his hold over the underworld.

Tonight, he mused, would be another step closer to that dream.

"How do you feel? Bloody wonderful, I bet!" Mitchell grinned as 'Morrissey' stepped into the foyer of Hendry Hall.

'Morrissey' reached up and peeled away the fake cold sore that adorned his lip. "It was thrilling," he admitted, "But I was terrified, too. That Horseman... I kept picturing him killing people like he did that night!"

Mitchell nodded, knowing that Cedric was still new to the dangerous lifestyle that they had all embraced. "Nobody tailed you back here?"

"I'm positive they didn't. Charon didn't act like he had any inkling that I wasn't who I appeared to be."

The two men entered the study, where they found Charity and Li waiting for them.

"The man's a natural," Mitchell said.

"So they took the bait?" Charity asked, looked relieved. She'd been very worried about Cedric's safety – but he and Li continued to emerge unscathed from the worst of situations.

"Definitely! Charon tried to pass it off as not being the sort of thing he went in for but I could see his eyes light up!"

Charity smiled. They'd used the information she'd gained from Dash to get a message to Charon – when the crime lord had sent word that he wanted to meet with Morrissey, she'd formulated a plan to use Cedric as their mouthpiece. "Good work," she said.

Cedric took a small bow. "My mother wanted me to be an actor, you know."

"A shame you've wasted your thespian abilities trying to seduce women," Li said with an amused grin.

"There are worse ways to spend an evening," he countered.

Mitchell looked at Charity, who had crossed over to a table where an array of weapons had been laid out. "The boat's ready whenever we are. I have it anchored far enough offshore to avoid detection."

"We'll stick with the plan, then. I want you and Cedric onboard and in disguise. In the dark, you can both pass for members of The Ten Fingers – I don't plan to let anyone get close enough to tell the difference."

"What about me?" Li asked.

Charity looked at her. "You'll be here, manning the phones. If we don't make it back by morning, you're to call Lazarus Gray and then

The Rook. Tell them that something's gone wrong and pass on all the info we have on Charon and the Horseman."

Li looked disappointed to be given phone duty but she also recognized the meaning behind Charity's words: she was basically leaving Li as the person who would continue their work if they all ended up dead.

Turning back to the weapons arrayed on the table, Charity picked up a sword and tested its weight. "I'm going to finish what you started, Mortimer. You have my word."

———— ∞ ————

Sovereign City Harbor was one of the busiest parts of the metropolis but it was also amongst the seediest. Wharf 18 was the worst of the worst and most honest sailors avoided the area like the plague. Nobody wanted to be associated with it. Back in '34, Doc Daye had temporarily brought about its closure, after busting a white slavery ring that was taking girls into and out of the city via the shipping lanes. But by late '35, it was operational again – and was once again home to the vilest trafficking imaginable.

Charon stepped out of the back seat of a black sedan, joined quickly by five of his best men. The Horseman arrived a moment later, the clop-clop of his steed's hooves sounding very loud on this quiet night.

"I think I see the boat," one of the men said, squinting off into the distance. "Can't wait to fill those chinks full of lead. Thought of them horning in on our city drives me nuts."

"It may be a cesspool but it's our cesspool," Charon muttered under his breath. The men didn't hear him, which was fine – he preferred to keep up his bluff of being some sort of occult figure. It was usually easy enough to do, given the presence of the Horseman.

The Horseman dismounted and the steed vanished in a shadowy mist. "Something is not right," the Hessian said.

"What do you mean?" Charon asked sharply, having learned to trust the instincts of this killing machine.

"I sense a familiar presence."

"If it's Cord, he's going to regret it," Charon whispered. "That bastard busted me a few years back – then laughed at me when I tried to bribe him! That's why I wanted his name smeared."

"It's not the police officer," the Horseman replied. His shoulders turned, as if his non-existent head was looking for the source of what he felt. He jerked as something whizzed past him, landing in the back of a goon's neck. It was a crossbow bolt and the other gunmen unleashed a torrent of obscenities as their friend fell to the ground, bleeding out.

"Up there!" one of them shouted and all eyes turned to the rooftop of a nearby warehouse. The silhouetted figure of Gravedigger stood there, which prompted the men to begin firing all of their guns in her direction. The bullets riddled the figure and finally knocked it down but there were no cries of pain, as would have been expected.

"It's a trap," Charon whispered. "That was a dummy or something!"

As if confirmation of this, two more crossbow bolts flew into the mob, taking two more men down to the ground. From the shadows, she jumped, sword whistling through the air. It swiped down, removing the head of the group's resident racist. As she landed in a crouch, she shoved the weapon back behind her, gutting the last of the gunmen.

In less than thirty seconds, she had killed five men, leaving behind only Charon and The Horseman.

"Kill her!" Charon shrieked. He shoved the Horseman's back, trying in vain to push the undead warrior towards Gravedigger.

"No."

Charon stared in fury at the Horseman. "What do you mean, 'no'?"

"I wish to see what she will do to you. And then I will finally face someone worthy of me."

Charon's head whipped back around. Gravedigger was walking towards him, sword in hand. A coil of intestine dangled from its tip and she shook it off with a quick flick of her wrist.

Charon started to run but his shoe caught on the hem of his robe, causing him to stagger. When he regained his footing, Gravedigger was upon him.

"Aren't you going to use your mystic powers to stop me?" she asked.

Raising his hands protectively, Nipper began the final scene of his life. He gesticulated in the air, chanting nonsense words in the hope that she would be frightened away.

Instead, Gravedigger laughed merrily, an insane sound that left Charon wailing in terror. Then her sword cut – once, twice and then a third time. The villain tumbled back, blood spurting from his wounds.

"He was beneath you," she said, turning back to The Headless Horseman. He had drawn his blade now and his stance indicated that he was excited by the prospect of combat.

"I agree. But I needed assistance in finding a place in this world.

Having seen more of it, however, I realize that nothing has truly changed. Man is still motivated by greed and lust. I can flourish here."

"I'm afraid you can't," she answered. "You've shown no inclination to be anything less than an unrepentant killer. That means I'm going to have to stop you."

"I am immune to death."

"I hurt you back at Hendry Hall. That's why you fled... and that's why you've been stopped before. Maybe all I'll do is drive you back into whatever hellish dimension you call home until you're summoned again... but I'll take that."

The Headless Horseman loomed over her, the foul odor that emanated from his wound intensifying. "You and I are not so dissimilar. We both crave the violence. And we both enjoy the kill."

"I only slay people who need to die – criminals and scum."

"No one is innocent. All men are fated to die."

"Let's agree to disagree, then." Gravedigger dropped into a battle stance. "Only one of us is walking away from this."

The Hessian drew his sword. "You are a brave woman – the bravest I have ever faced."

"Flattery's going to get you nowhere."

Gravedigger struck first.

"I hate this."

Mitchell didn't bother looking at Cedric. He knew what the other man meant and shared the sentiment. Instead, he continued watching through his binoculars, silently cheering as Charity stabbed The Hessian through the midsection. The blow wouldn't fell the undead warrior but it might slow him down, nonetheless.

"Seriously, can't we do something?"

"Like what?"

"I don't know – hurry the boat to the dock and join in? Or just start shooting from here?"

"We're still too far away – we'd just be wasting ammo and attracting attention. And even with the engines opened up full blast, the fight's liable to be over by the time we get to shore." Mitchell lowered his binoculars. "Charity has to do this by herself. She thinks she screwed up with Meeks and with the Hendry Hall affair. She needs a straight up victory."

Cedric lit a cigarette and exhaled. His nervousness was palpable. Despite the fact that Mitchell hid it well, he was just as bad. He thought of Charity as a close friend – and maybe, just maybe, a little bit more besides.

"You got a spare?" Mitchell asked.

"Didn't know you smoked."

"I don't. But I think I'm going to start."

Gravedigger grunted as The Horseman's blade crashed down upon her own. His strength was incredible and even with all the skills she had to draw upon, the battle was looking a bit one-sided. Her only hope lay in wounding him in his weak spot – the gory wound where his head had once resided. But reaching that spot was proving harder than she'd anticipated.

"Surrender, girl… and I'll make it quick."

"Please. You'd be so disappointed if I did that, you'd probably torture me for days just to spite me for ruining your fun."

"This is true."

The Hessian swung his weapon in a wide arc, allowing Gravedigger to duck under the blow. She grabbed the hilt of her own sword with both hands and drove it forward with all the strength she could muster. The blade sliced through his genitals and scraped against the pubic bone.

The Horseman's reaction was to grunt and strike her on the side of her shoulder with a closed fist.

Gravedigger grimaced. Her entire arm was tingling now. She sprang back from him, executing a series of flips that would have been the envy of any gymnast. She came to a stop just short of Charon's sedan. Leaping atop it, she tensed as The Horseman barreled towards her.

The villain's weapon whipped towards her but Gravedigger jumped upwards, over the attack. She then raised her weapon and speared it into his neck. The effect was immediate, as The Hessian snarled and backed away, gloved hands reaching ineffectually for the embedded sword.

Gravedigger drew a dagger, planning to continue her assault before he managed to rid himself of the painful implement. She spun the knife through the air and stabbed her foe. The Horseman grunted and twisted his body, preventing the weapon from striking his neck wound. It ended up in his shoulder, where it spent only a few seconds before Gravedigger yanked it free.

The Horseman caught her with a kick to the midsection, following it up with a punch to the top of her head. She staggered under the blow and was unable to avoid his sword, which caught her in her right hip. Blood flowed freely from the wound and Gravedigger knew that she was in danger of blacking out soon.

"I am more powerful than you," The Horseman said. He proved the point by punching her hard across the chin. The blow knocked her to her knees and left her ears ringing. He grabbed hold of the back of her hood and yanked her head up. His sword flashed against her throat, stopping just short of drawing blood. "I admire your bravery, however. At the last moment, even my stoutest of enemies have the flash of terror in their eyes. Sometimes they even beg. But you are different."

"I've died already," she hissed. "There's nothing you can do that's going to top that."

"Let's see, shall we?" The Horseman asked. There was undeniable glee in his voice.

Gravedigger drove her elbow into her enemy's stomach but it failed to dislodge his grip on her. Desperate to prolong the battle, she slipped a hand into the top of her boot, grabbing hold of a small porcelain egg-shaped object. Yanking it free, she swung her arm up and slipped the object into the Hessian's pocket.

The Horseman backed away, dropping his grip on Gravedigger. He heard a ticking sound emanating from his pocket and he reached a gloved hand in to grab the foreign object. He had just touched it when the device exploded, delivering enough impact to blow a hole in The Hessian's side. Gore dripped in copious amounts and the white of his bones showed through the flesh.

Roaring, The Horseman swung his sword in a killing stroke, intending to slice straight through the top of her skull.

Gravedigger vaulted to the side, flipping through the air. She landed in a crouch, dagger at the ready. As The Horseman staggered to face her, she raised her right arm and fired a crossbow bolt. It pierced her foe's leg, pinning it to the warehouse wall behind him. A second bolt slid into place and it, too, was fired, trapping the villain's other leg. As he struggled to free himself, Gravedigger rose to her full height.

"Say goodbye to the mortal world," she hissed, breathing deeply. Her hand trembled slightly, not just from the loss of blood, but also from a rising excitement. A part of her did enjoy the fight, the kill or be killed nature of the conflict – in that regard, The Horseman was right. Now that she sensed victory within her grasp, an almost sexual lust was filling her limbs.

The Horseman ceased trying to free himself. He lowered his weapon and his shoulders squared. His injured side was twitching, the magic that healed nearly all his wounds moving too slowly to save him under these circumstances. "I salute you... but this is not the end for me. When you are nothing more than a vaguely remembered memory, I will return. I will kill anew."

"Give it a rest – and go back to hell," Gravedigger said. She jumped up, stabbing downward with a stroke that delivered her knife's blade deep into The Hessian's neck.

The Horseman's scream echoed throughout the city, waking those who slumbered and chilling the blood of Sovereign's fiercest. At 6196 Robeson Avenue, Lazarus Gray looked up from his work to experience an uncommon shiver... while Doc Daye momentarily lost his train of thought. Onboard The Heart of Fortune, McCall woke from a troubled sleep, visions of the undead filling his mind's eye.

Gravedigger hit the ground in a tumbling roll, coming up to find that her weapons lay before her. There was no sign of The Horseman's corpse, nothing to show that he had ever been in her midst gone, even, were his footprints and the blood he had spilled.

"Blood," Gravedigger whispered. She glanced down and saw that there was evidence of The Horseman's presence, after all. Her wounds, seeping great amount of her life's blood....

The world grew dim. In the distance, a man was calling her name.

The face of Josef Goldstein flickered before her eyes.

And then all was black.

———

The Voice filled her mind, drowning out all else. *You have done well but your journey has only begun. There are many in this city and this world that need judgment.*

Charity opened her eyes. She was resting on her knees, in a brightly lit room. The walls were decorated by a soft floral pattern and the floor was lined with lush carpet. She wore her Gravedigger uniform, though with her hood thrown back and her mask resting on the floor beside her.

Directly in front of her was an elaborate fountain, one that was shaped like a mountain, with a waterfall gently cascading down its surface. The entire display was nearly six feet high and half that across. The craftsmanship was so amazing that Charity felt that she could almost feel the cool breeze wafting off the water and hear the clip-clop of a mountain goat's hooves.

Tearing her gaze away from the work of art, she looked around in hopes of finding the source of The Voice. "Where am I?" she asked.

You are Outside.

Charity blinked in confusion. "Did I die again?"

You still live but you have been gravely injured. Your friends shall heal you so that your campaign may continue. We are pleased that you have formed these attachments, they speak well of you. You inspire others to greatness, just as you inspire terror in the hearts of criminals.

Charity looked down, taking a deep breath. "Josef... when he died, what became of his spirit?"

He had long ago atoned for his sins. He has joined The Multitude.

So many confusing words and concepts, Charity thought. Will it ever make sense? Or am I doomed to not understanding – clarity only coming when I'm dead like Josef?

"What should I do next?" she asked.

Go back to your friends and continue the good work. The final member of your group is soon to arrive and then all will be in readiness. But know that every Gravedigger has an opposite and that you will recognize them when they are near. The Opposite will pose the greatest threat to you and the world.

"The opposite?" she asked aloud.

The room around her began to shimmer and the sounds of the fountain began to fade. Charity tried to stand up, not wanting to leave yet, not wanting to return without knowing about this 'opposite' or what new member of her group was soon to appear. Dizziness washed over her and she was unable to make it to her feet....

The words of The Voice came to her, as if from a great distance: *Stay true to your mission. The time for final judgment will come and when it does, you must not be found wanting.*

Charity opened her eyes, finding herself staring at the ceiling of her bedroom in Hendry Hall. For a moment, she wondered why she was here and then she remembered the group's decision to move their base of operations from Josef's house to Cedric's. It startled her to think about how she missed the other home – but this was both larger and safer.

She swung her legs over the edge of the bed, slipping her feet into a pair of comfy slippers. She wore only a nightshirt and she wondered with some amusement who had stripped her – hopefully it was Li, though she wouldn't have put it past Mitchell to do so. He was too much of a gentleman to have taken any liberties with her body but she still hoped that he hadn't seen her in that condition.

Memories of her final battle with the Horseman came rushing back but she pushed them aside after checking the bandage over her wound. It felt sore to the touch but she could tell it was healing already.

Of greater concern to her were the things that The Voice had said – words like The Multitude and The Opposite filled her with curiosity. She desperately wished that she could have spent more time Outside. Was that the home place of The Voice? Was it Heaven or some equivalent?

Charity got dressed while she contemplated these things. There were voices drifting up from down below and after putting on a soft blue dress and calf-high boots, she headed to join them

Mitchell and Cedric were seated in front of the fireplace, engaged in a competitive game of chess, while Li was flipping through a French fashion magazine. The young beauty was on the couch, her long legs tucked beneath her.

"Miss me?" Charity asked as she entered the study.

Li sprang from the couch and gave her a hug. "Sleeping beauty awakes!" she shouted happily.

Charity laughed and squeezed her friend. "How long was I out?"

"Not long. A week. Maybe a month."

Mitchell and Cedric approached, equally happy to see her back on her feet.

"It wasn't that long, luv. About eighteen hours."

"Who dressed my wound?"

"That was me," Li confirmed. "Dressed the wound, undressed the girl."

"Lucky you," Cedric muttered with a playful grin.

Mitchell gave him a nudge with his elbow and Cedric pretended to have taken a much larger blow, staggering back.

Li glanced at Charity and rolled her eyes in mock annoyance. "So, Chief, what's next?"

Charity took a deep breath before answering. "I think… I think we should all go out for a nice dinner."

"You're leaving your crypt, my dead friend?" Li teased. "I don't think you've been out without your mask for any length of time since you were buried in the dirt!"

"Did I ever tell you how I love your ability to frame a scene, Li?"

"No."

"That's because you don't have one." Charity shook her head. "We've done a good job. Let's celebrate. Josef left me enough money that I probably won't ever spend it so we might as well enjoy it from time to time."

Cedric nodded. "As long as I can pick up the gratuity."

"Mr. Moneybags likes to spend money, too," Li pointed out.

Mitchell noticed that Charity's expression was one of distraction. "Something bothering you?" he asked.

"I heard The Voice again," she admitted. "It told me a few things that didn't make much sense… it warned me that I had an enemy out there that it called The Opposite. And it also made it sound like there was going to be one more member of our group."

"Can't say that I consider either of those things to be good news," Cedric said. "Last thing we need is another enemy – and I quite like the group as it's currently constituted."

"We liked the group before you were added," Mitchell countered, "but we've warmed to you. We shouldn't dismiss more help out of hand."

A knocking from the front door made everyone pause. Since Cedric had yet to replace the help, he gave a smile and said, "I'll be right back."

"No." Charity stopped him with a touch to his arm. "Let me."

Cedric's eyes narrowed. "Expecting someone?"

"Could be our newest friend." *Or enemy*, she thought.

Charity left the room, aware of her friends' gaze upon her. Most acutely, she felt the burning stare of Mitchell. She wondered if it was wise to pursue any kind of relationship with him. The problems that his race presented couldn't be easily ignored, though she had no qualms about it personally. Others would, however, and that warranted concern. Additionally, there was the fact that they would be working very closely together – what if things turned south? How would it impact their ability to function as a unit?

She tensed as she reached the front door, readying herself for anything. Yanking the door open, she was prepared for any potential threat.

What she saw, however, gave her pause. There was a man standing there, evidently in his mid-thirties from the look of him. He was tall and well formed, with a rangy build that was quite pleasing in appearance. His eyes reflected a dark humor and ample intelligence.

"Can I help you?" she asked, involuntarily relaxing. There was something about this person that set her at ease, as if she had met him before.

"I hope so," he said, offering her a hand. "My name is Mortimer Quinn."

GRAVE MATTERS
OR...
HOW I CAME TO WRITE THIS BOOK

Hello, Faithful Readers! I hope you enjoyed the introduction to Gravedigger, the newest member of my New Pulp universe that began with the arrival of The Rook. Since The Rook's first flight back in 2008, I've added to the universe with Lazarus Gray, The Dark Gentleman, Guan-Yin, The Claws of The Rook and many more.

But none of them are quite like Gravedigger.

To understand how and why I created the character, we first have to go back to the misty past. It was a time of optimism and a surging economy. We were well on the way to electing the first Democratic President since Jimmy Carter. Grunge was filtering its way into the public consciousness.

It was 1992. I was 20 years old and in college, where I was working towards an undergraduate degree in Psychology. Then, as now, I was a huge comic book fan. Then, as now, I was a huge fan of the Valiant Universe. I loved the tight continuity it possessed and the way that little background events and characters would float from book to book, building a cohesive universe.

One of my favorite characters in that universe was Shadowman, who debuted in May 1992. A supernatural hero, Jack Boniface was poisoned by an alien, allowing him to "die" before being resurrected as an avenger of the night. We would later find out that he was only the latest in a long line of Shadowmen. I loved the concept and the series but it eventually faded away with the rest of the Valiant Universe.

But like all good things, it would not stay dead. Shadowman and the rest of the Valiant heroes were recently revived by a new Valiant. The promo art by Patrick Zircher floated around for months before the first issue actually debuted and I adored the revised look of the hero. It got me to thinking… Perhaps I needed to add a new title to my pulp hero collection, one that would serve as a "connector" series. It would have ties to all that had come before and would be the place where fans of The Rook or Lazarus Gray could come to get a taste of the greater universe.

I decided I wanted to make the new character a female, to balance out the male-heavy universe that I already had, and that I wanted her to be heavily supernatural as a nod to Shadowman. Like Jack, she would be the latest in a long line of heroes and, as with Shadowman and Lazarus Gray, rebirth would factor large in her origin.

From there, artist George Sellas and I tossed a few ideas back and forth. I had the name Gravedigger but I was afraid it was too masculine for Charity. He convinced me that it could be a neat twist on the name and concept. I told him my idea of tying Charity's past to Samantha Grace's origin, which he liked. It not only provided a link to the Lazarus series but also furthered the Grace family's role in the overall universe.

Once I'd come up with the full origin and George had done his initial character sketch, I thought it would be fun to have a "hand-off" in the story. When I wrote my first Lazarus Gray collection, The Rook appeared, as if giving his stamp of approval on the new arrival. With this one, I wanted to have both The Rook and Lazarus appear in ways that would bolster Gravedigger but not detract from her starring role. I was inspired by the way Star Trek used to do this – Dr McCoy from the original series was on the first episode of Next Generation, then Captain Picard from The Next Generation appeared on the first episode of Deep Space Nine, while that space station was a jumping-off point for Star Trek: Voyager when that series began. I thought was a nice wink and nod to the fans.

The decision to use The Headless Horseman in the book came about because I recycle everything. A few years ago, I wrote nearly 20,000 words on a novel I was going to call "Headless." It was going to be a sequel to Washington Irving's classic and would introduce a new hero of mine, Mortimer Quinn. I eventually abandoned the project but I always wanted to use parts of that story… so it ended up here. Tying Mortimer to the Gravedigger legacy was easy enough and allowed me to bring the Horseman into the story.

As for Charity's allies… one thing that I learned from the Lazarus Gray series is that I like having a steady cast of characters to supplement my protagonist. But I didn't want to create another Assistance Unlimited, who was inspired by Justice, Inc. Instead, I looked to another favorite pulp hero of mine – The Shadow. While Lazarus has a group of partners, The Shadow had a group of agents. There was never any doubt that Harry Vincent and Burbank were lower-ranking than The Shadow. That's what I set out to do here – Mitchell, Cedric and Li all get their 'origins' here and we see what skills they bring to the table. All of them, however, are agents – not partners. Our heroine is the one that stands on center stage during the final conflict.

So where do we go from here? Obviously, the arrival of Mortimer on the last page suggests that there are more stories to be told here. This first Gravedigger novel will appear in 2013 and I hope to follow with a second volume in 2014, if the fates are with me. I hope to continue to update her adventures regularly, just as I have with Lazarus and The Rook.

Stop by my blog (http://www.barryreese.net) to keep up with the goings-on in all my pulp stories, as well as take a gander at exclusive artwork.

Speaking of artwork, I have to say thank you to George Sellas, for designing Gravedigger's look and for the incredibly awesome cover he whipped up. Also, Will Meugniot's interior illustrations perfectly captured the mood of the story, pairing Charity's obvious beauty with her deadly nature. Thanks, guys.

Lock your doors, everyone. Gravedigger is hitting the streets.

THE UNIVERSE ACCORDING TO BARRY REESE
A TIMELINE
by Barry Reese

Major Events specific to certain stories and novels are included in brackets. Some of this information contains SPOILERS for The Rook, Lazarus Gray, Eobard Grace and other stories.

~ 800 Viking warrior Grimarr dies of disease but is resurrected as the Sword of Hel. He adventures for some time as Hel's agent on Earth. *["Dogs of War" and "In the Name of Hel," Tales of the Norse Gods].*

1748 - Johann Adam Weishaupt is born.

1750 - Guan-Yin embarks on a quest to find her lost father, which takes her to Skull Island *[Guan-Yin and the Horrors of Skull Island].*

1776 - Johann Adam Weishaupt forms The Illuminati. He adopts the guise of the original Lazarus Gray in group meetings, reflecting his "rebirth" and the "moral ambiguity" of the group. In Sovereign City, a Hessian soldier dies in battle, his spirit resurrected as an headless warrior.

1793 - Mortimer Quinn comes to Sovereign City, investigating the tales of a Headless Horseman *[Gravedigger Volume One]*

1865 - Eobard Grace returns home from his actions in the American Civil War. Takes possession of the Book of Shadows from his uncle Frederick. *["The World of Shadow," The Family Grace: An Extraordinary History]*

1877 - Eobard Grace is summoned to the World of Shadows, where he battles Uris-Kor and fathers a son, Korben. *["The World of Shadow," The Family Grace: An Extraordinary History]*

1885 - Along with his niece Miriam and her paramour Ian Sinclair, Eobard returns to the World of Shadows to halt the merging of that world with Earth. *["The Flesh Wheel," The Family Grace: An Extraordinary History]*

1890 - Eobard fathers a second son, Leopold.

1895 - Felix Cole (the Bookbinder) is born.

1900 - Max Davies is born to publisher Warren Davies and his wife, heiress Margaret Davies.

1901 - Leonid Kaslov is born.

1905 - Richard Winthrop is born in San Francisco.

1908 - Warren Davies is murdered by Ted Grossett, a killer nicknamed "Death's Head". *["Lucifer's Cage", the Rook Volume One, more details shown in "Origins," the Rook Volume Two]* Hans Merkel kills his own father. *["Blitzkrieg," the Rook Volume Two]*

1910 - Evelyn Gould is born.

1913 - Felix Cole meets the Cockroach Man and becomes part of The Great Work. *["The Great Work," The Family Grace: An Extraordinary History]*

1914 - Margaret Davies passes away in her sleep. Max is adopted by his uncle Reginald.

1915 - Felix Cole marries Charlotte Grace, Eobard Grace's cousin.

1916 - Leonid Kaslov's father Nikolai becomes involved in the plot to assassinate Rasputin.

1917 - Betsy Cole is born to Felix and Charlotte Grace Cole. Nikolai Kaslov is murdered.

1918 - Max Davies begins wandering the world. Richard Winthrop's parents die in an accident.

1922 - Warlike Manchu tutors Max Davies in Kyoto.

1925 - Max Davies becomes the Rook, operating throughout Europe.

1926 - Charlotte Grace dies. Richard Winthrop has a brief romance with exchange student Sarah Dumas.

1927 - Richard Winthrop graduates from Yale. On the night of his graduation, he is recruited into The Illuminati. Max and Leopold Grace battle the Red Lord in Paris. Richard Winthrop meets Miya Shimada in Japan, where he purchases The McGuinness Obelisk for The Illuminati.

1928 - The Rook returns to Boston. Dexter van Melkebeek (later to be known as The Darkling) receives his training in Tibet from Tenzin.

1929 - Max Davies is one of the judges for the Miss Beantown contest *["The Miss Beantown Affair," Tales of the Rook]*. Richard Winthrop destroys a coven of vampires in Mexico.

1930 - Richard Winthrop pursues The Devil's Heart in Peru *["Eidolon," Lazarus Gray Volume Three]*.

1932 - The Rook hunts down his father's killer *["Origins," the Rook Volume Two]*. The Darkling returns to the United States.

1933 - Jacob Trench uncovers Lucifer's Cage. *["Lucifer's Cage", the Rook Volume One]* The Rook battles Doctor York *[All-Star Pulp Comics # 1]* After a failed attempt at betraying The Illuminati, Richard Winthrop wakes up on the shores of Sovereign City with no memory of his name or past. He has only one clue to his past in his possession: a small medallion adorned with the words Lazarus Gray and the image of a naked man with the head of a lion. *["The Girl With the Phantom Eyes," Lazarus Gray Volume One]*

1934 - Now calling himself Lazarus Gray, Richard Winthrop forms Assistance Unlimited in Sovereign City. He recruits Samantha Grace, Morgan Watts and Eun Jiwon *["The Girl With the Phantom Eyes," Lazarus Gray Volume One]* Walther Lunt aids German scientists in unleashing the power Die Glocke, which in turn frees the demonic forces of Satan's Circus *["Die Glocke," Lazarus Gray Volume Two]*. The entity who will become known as The Black Terror is created *["The Making of a Hero," Lazarus Gray Volume Two]*.

1935 - Felix Cole and his daughter Betsy seek out the Book of Eibon. ["The Great Work," The Family Grace: An Extraordinary History] Assistance Unlimited undertakes a number of missions, defeating the likes of Walther Lunt, Doc Pemberley, Malcolm Goodwill & Black Heart, Princess Femi & The Undying, Mr. Skull, The Axeman and The Yellow Claw *["The Girl With the Phantom Eyes," "The Devil's Bible," "The Corpse Screams at Midnight," "The Burning Skull," "The Axeman of Sovereign City," and "The God of Hate," Lazarus Gray Volume One]* The Rook journeys to Sovereign City and teams up with Assistance Unlimited to battle Devil Face *["Darkness, Spreading Its Wings of Black," the Rook Volume Six)]*. Lazarus Gray and Assistance Unlimited become embroiled in the search for Die Glocke *["Die Glocke," Lazarus Gray Volume Two]*

1936 - Assistance Unlimited completes their hunt for Die Glocke and confronts the threat of Jack-In-Irons. Abigail Cross and Jakob Sporrenberg join Assistance Unlimited *["Die Glocke," Lazarus Gray Volume Two]*. The Rook moves to Atlanta and recovers the Dagger of Elohim from Felix Darkholme. The Rook meets Evelyn Gould. The Rook battles Jacob Trench. *["Lucifer's Cage", the Rook Volume One]*. Reed Barrows revives Camilla. *["Kingdom of Blood," The Rook Volume One]*. Kevin Atwill is abandoned in the Amazonian jungle by his friends, a victim of the Gorgon legacy. *["The Gorgon Conspiracy," The Rook Volume Two]*. Nathaniel Caine's lover is killed by Tweedledum while

Dan Daring looks on *["Catalyst," The Rook Volume Three]* Assistance Unlimited teams up with The Black Terror to battle Promethus and The Titan in South America *["The Making of a Hero," Lazarus Gray Volume Two]*. Doc Pemberley allies himself with Abraham Klee, Stanley Davis and Constance Majestros to form Murder Unlimited. Lazarus Gray is able to defeat this confederation of evil and Pemberley finds himself the victim of Doctor Satan's machinations *["Murder Unlimited," Lazarus Gray Volume Three]*. Lazarus Gray is forced to compete with The Darkling for possession of a set of demonic bones. During the course of this, a member of Assistance Unlimited becomes Eidolon. *["Eidolon," Lazarus Gray Volume Three]*. Charity Grace dies and is reborn as the first female Gravedigger. *[Gravedigger Volume One]*

1937 - Max and Evelyn marry. Camilla attempts to create Kingdom of Blood. World's ancient vampires awaken and the Rook is 'marked' by Nyarlathotep. Gerhard Klempt's experiments are halted. William McKenzie becomes Chief of Police in Atlanta. The Rook meets Benson, who clears his record with the police. *["Kingdom of Blood," the Rook Volume One]*. Lazarus Gray and Assistance Unlimited teams up with Thunder Jim Wade to confront the deadly threat of Leviathan *[("Leviathan Rising", Lazarus Gray Volume Four]*. Hank Wilbon is murdered, leading to his eventual resurrection as the Reaper. *["Kaslov's Fire," The Rook Volume Two]*. The Rook and Evelyn become unwelcome guests of Baron Werner Prescott, eventually foiling his attempts to create an artificial island and a weather-controlling weapon for the Nazis *["The Killing Games," Tales of the Rook]* Gravedigger confronts a series of terrible threats in Sovereign City, including Thanatos, a gender-swapping satanic cult and The Headless Horseman. Charity and Samantha Grace make peace about their status as half-sisters. *[Gravedigger Volume One]* Lazarus Gray teams with Eidolon and The Darkling to combat Doctor Satan *["Satan's Circus," Lazarus Gray Volume Four]*

1938 - The Rook travels to Great City to aid the Moon Man in battling Lycos and his Gasping Death. The Rook destroys the physical shell of Nyarlathotep and gains his trademark signet ring. *["The Gasping Death," The Rook Volume One]*. The jungle hero known as the Revenant is killed *["Death from the Jungle," The Rook Volume Four]*

1939 - Ibis and the Warlike Manchu revive the Abomination. Evelyn becomes pregnant and gives birth to their first child, a boy named William. *["Abominations," The Rook Volume One]*. The Rook allies himself with Leonid Kaslov to stop the Reaper's attacks and to foil the plans of Rasputin. *["Kaslov's Fire," the Rook Volume Two]* Violet Cambridge and Will McKenzie become embroiled in the hunt for a mystical item known as The Damned Thing *[The Damned Thing]*

1940 - The Warlike Manchu returns with a new pupil -- Hans Merkel, aka Shinigami. The Warlike Manchu kidnaps William Davies but the Rook and Leonid Kaslov manage to rescue the boy. *["Blitzkrieg," the Rook Volume Two]* The Rook journeys to Germany alongside the Domino Lady and Will McKenzie to combat the demonic organization known as Bloodwerks. *["Bloodwerks," the Rook Volume Two]* Kevin Atwill seeks revenge against his former friends, bringing him into conflict with the Rook *["The Gorgon Conspiracy," The Rook Volume Two]*. The Rook takes a young vampire under his care, protecting him from a cult that worships a race of beings known as The Shambling Ones. With the aid of Leonid Kazlov, the cult is destroyed *["The Shambling Ones," The Rook Volume Two]*.

1941 - Philip Gallagher, a journalist, uncovers the Rook's secret identity but chooses to become an ally of the vigilante rather than reveal it to the world *["Origins," the Rook Volume Two]*. The Rook teams with the Black Bat and Ascott Keane, as well as a reluctant Doctor Satan, in defeating the plans of the sorcerer Arias *["The Bleeding Hells"]*. The Rook rescues McKenzie from the Iron Maiden *["The Iron Maiden," The Rook Volume Three]*.

1942 - The Rook battles a Nazi super agent known as the Grim Reaper, who is attempting to gather the Crystal Skulls *["The Three Skulls," The Rook Volume Three]*. The Rook becomes embroiled in a plot by Sun Koh and a group of Axis killers known as The Furies. The Rook and Sun Koh end up in deadly battle on the banks of the Potomac River. *["The Scorched God," The Rook Volume Six]*. In London, the Rook and Evelyn meet Nathaniel Caine (aka the Catalyst) and Rachel Winters, who are involved in stopping the Nazis from creating the Un-Earth. They battle Doctor Satan and the Black Zeppelin *["Catalyst," The Rook*

Volume Three]. Evelyn learns she's pregnant with a second child. The Rook solves the mystery of the Roanoke Colony *["The Lost Colony," The Rook Volume Three]*. The Rook battles against an arsonist in the employ of Bennecio Tommasso *["Where There's Smoke", Tales of the Rook]*. The Warlike Manchu is revived and embarks upon a search for the Philosopher's Stone *["The Resurrection Gambit," The Rook Volume Three]*

1943 - The Rook teams with Xander to deal with the Onyx Raven *["The Onyx Raven, Tales of the Rook]*. The Rook is confronted by the twin threats of Fernando Pasarin and the undead pirate Hendrik van der Decken *["The Phantom Vessel," The Rook Volume Four]*. Evelyn and Max become the parents of a second child, Emma Davies. The Rook teams with the daughter of the Revenant to battle Hermann Krupp and the Golden Goblin *["Death from the Jungle," The Rook Volume Four]* The Rook battles Doctor Satan over possession of an ancient Mayan tablet *["The Four Rooks," The Rook Volume Four]*. The Rook travels to Peru to battle an undead magician called The Spook *["Spook," The Rook Volume Four]*. The Rook clashes with Doctor Death, who briefly takes possession of Will McKenzie *["The Rook Nevermore," Tales of the Rook]*. Baron Rudolph Gustav gains possession of the Rod of Aaron and kidnaps Evelyn, forcing the Rook into an uneasy alliance with the Warlike Manchu *["Dead of Night," The Rook Volume Four]*. Doctor Satan flees to the hidden land of Vorium, where the Rook allies with Frankenstein's Monster to bring him to justice *["Satan's Trial," The Rook Volume Four]*. Tim Roland is recruited by The Flame and Miss Masque *["The Ivory Machine," The Rook Volume Five]*. The Black Terror investigates a German attempt to replicate his powers and becomes friends with a scientist named Clarke ["Terrors"]

1944 - The Rook organizes a strike force composed of Revenant, Frankenstein's Monster, Catalyst and Esper. The group is known as The Claws of the Rook and they take part in two notable adventures in this year: against the diabolical Mr. Dee and then later against an alliance between Doctor Satan and the Warlike Manchu *["The Diabolical Mr. Dee" and "A Plague of Wicked Men", The Rook Volume Five]*.

1946 - The Rook discovers that Adolph Hitler is still alive and has become a vampire in service to Dracula. In an attempt to stop the villains from using the Holy Lance to take over the world, the Rook allies with the Claws of the Rook, a time traveler named Jenny Everywhere, a thief called Belladonna and Leonid Kaslov. The villains are defeated and Max's future is revealed to still be in doubt. Events shown from 2006 on are just a possible future. The Rook also has several encounters with a demonically powered killer known as Stickman. *["The Devil's Spear," The Rook Volume Five]*. The Rook encounters a madman named Samuel Garibaldi (aka Rainman) and his ally, Dr. Gottlieb Hochmuller. The Rook and his Claws team defeat the villainous duo and several new heroes join the ranks of the Claws team -- Miss Masque, Black Terror & Tim and The Flame. *["The Ivory Machine," The Rook Volume Five]*

1953 - The Rook acquires the Looking Glass from Lu Chang. *["Black Mass," The Rook Volume One]*

1961 - Max's son William becomes the second Rook. *["The Four Rooks," The Rook Volume Four]*

1967 - The second Rook battles and defeats the Warlike Manchu, who is in possession of the Mayan Tablet that Doctor Satan coveted in '43. Evelyn Davies dies. *["The Four Rooks," The Rook Volume Four]*

1970 - William Davies (the second Rook) commits suicide by jumping from a Manhattan rooftop. Emma Davies (Max's daughter and William's brother) becomes the Rook one week later, in February. *["The Four Rooks," The Rook Volume Four]*

1973 - The third Rook is accompanied by Kayla Kaslov (daughter of Leonid Kaslov) on a trip to Brazil, where the two women defeat the Black Annis and claim the Mayan Tablet that's popped up over the course of three decades. Emma gives it to her father, who in turn passes it on to Catalyst (Nathaniel Caine) *["The Four Rooks," The Rook Volume Four]*

~1985 - Max resumes operating as the Rook, adventuring sporadically. Due to various magical events, he remains far more active than most men his age. The reasons for Emma giving up the role are unknown at this time.

Events depicted in the years 2006 forward occur in one of many possible futures for The Rook. As revealed in Volume Five of The Rook Chronicles, the events of 2006 onward may -- or may not -- be the ultimate future of Max Davies.

2006 - The Black Mass Barrier rises, enveloping the world in a magical field. The World of Shadows merges with Earth. Fiona Grace (descended from Eobard) becomes a worldwide celebrity, partially due to her failure to stop the Black Mass Barrier. *["Black Mass," The Rook Volume One]*

2009 - Ian Morris meets Max Davies and becomes the new Rook. He meets Fiona Grace. Max dies at some point immediately following this. *["Black Mass," The Rook Volume One]*

2010 - The Ian Morris Rook and Fiona Grace deal with the threat of Baron Samedi *["The Curse of Baron Samedi," Tales of the Rook]*

2012 - The fourth Rook (Ian Morris) receives the Mayan Tablet from Catalyst, who tells him that the world will end on December 21, 2012 unless something is done. Using the tablet, Ian attempts to take control of the magic spell that will end the world. Aided by the spirits of the three previous Rooks, he succeeds, though it costs him his life. He is survived by his lover (Fiona Grace) and their unborn child. Max Davies is reborn as a man in his late twenties and becomes the Rook again. *["The Four Rooks," The Rook Volume Four]*

ABOUT THE AUTHOR

Barry Reese has spent the last decade writing for publishers as diverse as Marvel Comics, West End Games, Wild Cat Books and Moonstone Books. Known primarily for his pulp adventure works like The Rook Chronicles, The Adventures of Lazarus Gray and Savage Tales of Ki-Gor, Barry has also delved into slasher horror (Rabbit Heart) and even the fantasy pirate genre (Guan-Yin and the Horrors of Skull Island). His favorite classic pulp heroes are The Avenger, Doc Savage, John Carter, Conan and Seekay. More information about him can be found at **http://www.barryreese.net**

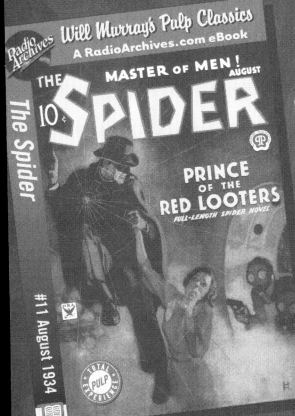

Made in the USA
Lexington, KY
07 April 2013